THE
SHADOWS *of* OWLSNAP

For five bridesmaids
Rebecca, Margaret, Matilda, Frances and Hannah

THE
SHADOWS of OWLSNAP

Angela Bull

DENT CHILDREN'S BOOKS · LONDON

Printed in Great Britain
for J. M Dent & Sons Ltd
91 Clapham High Street
London SW4 7TA

A catalogue for this book is available from
the British Library.

ISBN 0–460–88117–5

1

Everybody seemed to know that Quarmby Hall was haunted.

'How's the ghost?' the milkman asked, the morning after the Crofts moved in, before he'd even asked if they wanted eggs, yoghurts or fruit juices.

'Have you heard strange footsteps?' the lady in the village shop probed. 'Well, maybe you won't, though it's early days yet. I've got that big mirror you ordered, Mrs Croft. The van-man left it with me. He said your lane was too steep for his van, but I knew why he wouldn't deliver it. He's a nervous sort of chap.'

'There are tales,' the estate agent had remarked casually, when he was selling the house to the Crofts. 'But old houses attract spooky rumours.'

'Women in white, gliding through closed doors? Wailing nuns?' suggested Mrs Croft.

'Exactly.'

The estate agent grinned with relief. Quarmby Hall had remained unsold for a long time, and here at last was a family willing to risk buying it.

Probably it was the look of the house which made people think of ghosts. Quarmby Hall crouched alone, above the village, beside a steep lane running up on to the moors. Crooked roofs huddled secretively down over its dark stone walls. Deep-set windows lurked at queer heights and angles. One end was taller, with a high, pointed gable, so that from a distance the house had the air of a grazing animal, with chimneys for ears.

Around it stretched a wild, overgrown garden, with a few sagging ruins of barns and stables at the back. Somewhere, the estate agent told them, there was a legendary Bottomless Well; not really bottomless, of course, though certainly deep. But nowadays nobody could remember where it was.

The old house in its rugged setting caught the fancy of Mr and Mrs Croft. They were used to neat avenues of modern houses, where gardens frothed with flowering trees. Buying Quarmby Hall made them feel adventurous.

'You'll love it,' they told their children.

There were four children in the Croft family. Christopher and Nicola were the eldest; teenagers, tall, fair and self-confident. They wore the right clothes, did the right things, and had crowds of friends. Nine-year-old Louise enjoyed being the youngest. And between Nicola and Louise, came Alastair. He was twelve, and the clever member of the family. Not for him the toughness and trendiness adopted by Chris and Nicola, nor the petting which Louise enjoyed as the baby of the family. Alastair went his own way, and did his own thing.

Chris and Nicola crashed boldly into Quarmby Hall, ready for anything. Alastair and Louise were more hesitant.

'It's got no proper shape,' objected Alastair. He knew suddenly that he liked things to be orderly; houses rectangular, for instance, with sensible arrangements of upstairs and downstairs. Quarmby Hall was all jutting wings and random levels.

'It's like a maze. I'll get lost,' said Louise. The house wasn't so enormous, but it had a confusing jumble of rooms opening out of each other, and several narrow, crooked staircases.

'We'll soon straighten it out,' said their father. 'We'll

2

knock some walls down, and make one big sitting-room. And level off the floors too. The furniture's sliding all over the place.'

It certainly was. The floors and walls sloped this way and that, sending back dull wooden echoes of the family's clattering feet.

'I think it's gorgeous!' said their mother. And, with half the things still packed in boxes, she sat down with the postcards she had bought at the village shop and wrote, 'We've got this marvellous, ghost-ridden house!' to all the friends they had left behind in Surrey.

The village itself was picturesquely strung out along a winding lane, which had once been an important road from Yorkshire into Lancashire. A bypass took the traffic another way now; and the village, so the lady in the shop said, was full of artists and writers, soaking up its quaint charm.

As far as Alastair was concerned, Quarmby Hall had only one advantage over their old home – the children could each have their own bedroom. In Surrey they had shared in pairs.

Sorting out the bedrooms was quite a tricky job.

'I want somewhere that I can find, and that feels safe,' said Louise; choosing a tiny room beside her parents' bedroom, just at the top of the stairs leading up from the hall.

'I need something big,' announced Chris, who had a pool table and an exercise bike to accommodate. Luckily there was a big, sprawling, misshapen room at one end of the house which pleased him. 'Great for having friends round,' he remarked, surveying all the nooks and crannies happily.

Alastair was glad to find a plain, square bedroom next to Chris's, with a nearly-flat floor. He set up his computer, and arranged his big science encyclopedias along the carved mantlepiece.

'This'll be OK,' said Chris when he looked in on Alastair. 'We'll be well away from earfuls of piercing music.'

In their Surrey days Chris had often complained about the volume of Nicola's music. But now she had chosen a distant room, up three steps and along a twisting passage, where she could play her tapes as loudly as she liked.

Louise peeped into Nicola's bedroom.

'Won't you be scared here, away from us all?' she asked.

'Not likely!' said Nicola, who was blu-tacking posters, as well as she could, to the crooked, bulging walls. 'And if any ghosts come through one door, I'll escape by the other.'

Louise looked across at the second door.

'Where does it go?'

'On to a sort of landing, with two lots of stairs. One goes down to the passage by the kitchen, and one winds up to a funny little room, all by itself under the end gable. I'm calling it the Gable Room'

'It sounds horrid,' said Louise, but Nicola laughed, and said she thought a spooky old house was ace. She didn't mind that the bedrooms were scattered in separate corners and on different levels.

The family soon settled in to their new home. In spite of Mum's postcards, there were no signs of any ghosts. No eerie footsteps or melancholy wailings disturbed their nights, and the children slept comfortably in their separate bedrooms.

Downstairs, the big sitting-room that Dad had planned was opened up. One of the many larders, which spread like a honeycomb round the kitchen, was turned into a cloakroom, and in another, Dad arranged the

4

filing cabinets he needed for his job as marketing manager in a sports firm. Near the front door was a small study, which Mum, who was a teacher, had pounced on for herself. Mitt the Kitt, their tabby cat, had chosen the rug by the Aga as a special base.

Even when all this was settled, when the freezer and the washing machine, the tumble drier and the electronic keyboard, had been installed, there were still odd little empty rooms, waiting.

Alastair didn't like them – and then was annoyed with himself for being so gutless. What, after all, were rooms? Just gaps between a mesh of stone walls, which, in the case of Quarmby Hall, had been rather badly constructed. If he'd been the builder, he'd be ashamed of making such a pig's ear of the job.

Maybe it was the lack of a clear plan which gave the rooms that odd feeling.

Alastair scrubbed the word 'odd' from his mind, and substituted 'unsatisfactory' instead. 'Unsatisfactory workmanship.' A label like that made Quarmby Hall more manageable.

Chris and Nicola felt quite differently. To them, living in a house which might be haunted was a thrilling status symbol. Beginning at a new school in January was difficult, with classes already settled, and courses half-way through; but, as they explained to the rest of the family, a mention of ghosts soon drew a cluster of potential friends around them.

'I don't know how they can joke about ghosts,' said Louise to Alastair, as they slogged up the steep lane home from their own school one dismal afternoon. 'I mean, the ghosts might come and take revenge on them for showing off. I'd hate people showing off about me, if I was a ghost, wouldn't you? Alastair? Wouldn't you?'

'Oh, I dunno,' Alastair mumbled.

'Well, I would,' said Louise, and she began to run as a shower of sleety rain blew down from the moor into their faces.

It seemed as if there were drawbacks to their ghost boast, as Chris and Nicola revealed that evening.

'Everyone goes on so,' grumbled Nicola, as they sat round the table, under the low kitchen beams. 'I'm getting fed up.'

'Me too,' agreed Chris. 'I was in the shower after swimming today, and some idiot came leaping out at me, flapping a white towel and hooting.'

'This boy joined me in the dinner queue, and started talking,' Nicola went on. 'I thought he was going to chat me up; he was quite good-looking. But all he wanted was to snitch some ideas on the supernatural for a project he was doing. He wasn't interested in me at all.'

'I've changed my mind, anyway,' said Chris. 'I'm sure the house isn't haunted. None of us has seen a thing. I don't believe in ghosts.'

Nicola nodded. 'Yeah, it's all a load of rubbish. I wish I'd never said anything.'

'Hold on!' protested Mum. 'You may not have seen them, but that doesn't disprove their existence.'

'Oh, Mum!' Chris and Nicola groaned together.

'You're so romantic,' Nicola told her. 'Just because your Scottish ancestors had second sight.'

Louise looked up from her plate. 'I believe in ghosts,' she said.

Chris and Nicola eyed her pityingly, but Dad came to the rescue.

'Why d'you believe in them, Lou?'

'The dark corners,' said Louise. 'And when I'm in bed, I hear creaking.'

'Old houses always creak,' answered Dad, 'especially on a windy hillside like this.'

6

'Good! Dad's on our side, Chris,' said Nicola.

'Dad wouldn't believe in a ghost if it hit him on the nose with a rolling pin,' said Mum.

'Hey, I might!' said Dad.

'You wouldn't. But I'm on Louise's side,' said Mum. 'I think there might be ghosts, though I haven't seen any.'

Suddenly, they all looked at Alastair. He hadn't spoken. He was concentrating on his own thoughts while he ate. That was how it had been ever since they had moved in to Quarmby Hall. He found it the best way of coping with his creepy new surroundings. While Mum and Dad fussed over colour co-ordination, and bathroom conversions, and Chris and Nicola were busy elbowing their way into the world of sports and parties which they had enjoyed in Surrey, and Louise, thumb in mouth, curled up in front of countless videos, he kept his mind busy with knotty scientific problems. He pondered over what Time really was, and how the Big Bang happened.

'Do you believe in ghosts, Alastair?' Chris challenged.

Alastair paused. He didn't want to answer, but he couldn't avoid it.

'It depends what you mean by ghosts,' he stalled, and the others burst out laughing, Chris loudest of all.

'Everyone knows what ghosts are!' cried Nicola.

'Except brainbox Alastair Croft,' declared Chris. 'Come on, have you seen one?'

'No.' That was true enough.

'Good! Alastair's on our side. Four to two against you, Mum, I'm afraid.'

'Everyone in the village believes in them,' argued Mum.

'Then they'll have a chance to find out how wrong they've been when they come to our house-warming

7

party,' said Dad. 'We'll throw the house open – it'll be a good excuse to show what we've done. You kids can invite your friends, and there are people from the village I want to ask. I got chatting to an interesting bloke in the Fleece the other night, called Tony Elland. He knows the whole history of these parts. We'll give everyone a good supper, and if they can produce a ghost for us, so much the better.'

'Let's have chilli con carne,' begged Nicola.

'And jacket potatoes,' added Louise.

Once again, a hum of conversation covered Alastair's silence. He sat at the table, with them yet apart, his toes clenched inside his trainers.

Naturally his scientific mind doubted anything as ridiculously flimsy as a ghost. But somewhere amongst the rambling rooms of Quarmby Hall, he had, at moments, felt – what? Hardly more than a giddiness, a touch of licking chill. He'd shaken it off, surprising himself by not wanting to investigate; by fixing his thoughts, indeed, on other things, so that he was no longer exactly sure what he had encountered.

Now, suddenly, he couldn't stop wondering about all those dark little rooms, piled above and around them, untamed, in spite of the new colour schemes, Chris's laughter, and Nicola's music, where tendrils of old time might still coil . . .

He felt a stab of longing for the house they'd left behind in Surrey, with its straight staircase, and bright, ordinary rooms.

2

The house-warming party was in full swing. Firelight and lamplight threw the flickering shadows of the guests across the crooked walls of the big sitting-room. There were schoolfriends in their best gear, Dad's boss in his business suit, teachers Mum knew, and all sorts of village people, from the lady in the shop to shaggy-sweatered artists and writers. Dad poured drinks, the rest of the family passed snacks, and a babble of conversation rose above the soft thrumming of the hi-fi.

'So you haven't seen the ghost yet? Dearie me, I am surprised!' said the lady from the shop.

'No. It's very disappointing,' said Mum.

'But there are strange vibes in the house. I caught them as soon as I came in.'

Alastair, handing round peanuts, glanced sharply at the last speaker. It was Tony Elland, the 'interesting bloke' Dad had talked to in the local pub. He had a thin, inquiring face, rather like Sherlock Holmes.

'You must be psychic if you can detect strange vibes through the hullabaloo all these kids are making,' joked Dad.

'Hey, Dad!' protested Nicola.

'How do you mean, strange vibes?' asked Mum.

Several people besides Alastair were looking at Tony Elland now, and he backtracked, a little embarrassed.

'Oh, nothing really. Maybe evil influences are still drifting down from Whinnerah Clough.'

'What is Whinnerah Clough?' Mum wanted to know.

9

'It's on the signpost at the bottom of our lane, but with the weather being so nasty, no one's felt like exploring.'

'Whinnerah Clough itself is just a hollow in the hills.' Tony began, 'but there's a farm in it which was the home of a gang of yellow traders over two hundred years ago.'

Before he could say more, his words were drowned by a splurge of voices from Chris and his friends.

'Yeah, let's have a ghost-hunt!' Chris was exclaiming. 'It's time we tracked down the spooks. Mum, Dad! Some of us are going off ghost-hunting.'

'I'll be scared rotten!' squeaked one of the girls.

'No, it'll be brilliant!' cried another.

'Can we come too?' demanded the twins, Simon and Sukey.

They had been invited by Alastair, not because they were his special friends, but because they seemed to expect to be asked. His only other guest was a plumpish boy called Pete, who had attached himself to Alastair when he had arrived at the new school, perhaps because he was a bit of an outsider in the class himself.

'Anyone who's brave enough can come,' declared Nicola. Her eyes sparkled with excitement. 'But we'll have to go in the dark. No, hang on. Candles are allowed. I'll put some round the house.'

She dashed out of the room.

'It sounds very frightening,' quavered the lady from the shop.

'Oh, grown-ups aren't expected to come,' said Chris, quickly and firmly.

'You won't find anything,' warned Dad. 'There's nothing to be found. Who's ready for another drink?'

'I think I'll go and finish off the supper,' said Mum.

'We'll go ghost-hunting, won't we?' Pete said to Alastair.

'But not in pairs,' instructed Chris. 'Go on your own.'

And he herded the jostling bunch of schoolfriends into the hall, where pale candlelight swayed in the draught.

'Go wherever you want, but spread out well. Good hunting!' said Chris, as footsteps rattled away into the shadows.

Minutes later, Alastair hurried into the kitchen, letting the door bang behind him. In the passage outside he had scooped up Mitt the Kitt, and now he hugged her to his chest, in case the thumping of his heart was visible through his shirt.

The kitchen was brimming with light and warmth, a tasty, spicy smell – and safety! His mother and a History teacher from her school, a cheerful, grey-haired lady called Helen, were busy at the Aga. Helen was stirring a great pan of chilli con carne. Mum was getting out jacket potatoes, and pinching them to see if they were done.

'Feeling hungry?' she asked Alastair, with a smile.

He shook his head. If he told the truth, he would say he was feeling sick with shock, but the truth was impossible. What had happened was too frightening, and, at the same time, too vague, to put into words.

'I thought Mitt the Kitt might need feeding,' he said, and he began to clatter about with tins, and tin-openers, and bowls, hoping he looked normal, and not chalky white, as he might well do. Behind him, Mum and Helen were chatting.

'Another thing I keep wondering,' said Mum, 'is why the house is called Quarmby Hall. What does Quarmby mean?'

'It's a family name,' said Helen. 'The Quarmby family lived here for generations, and in those days the house was called Owl Snape. They came to grief about 1760, and much later the name was changed to Quarmby Hall.

To remember them by, I suppose.'

'What do you mean – came to grief?' asked Mum, clearly thrilled by this dramatic phrase.

'The last of them, Thomas Quarmby, gambled everything away on cock-fighting,' Helen explained.

'Cock-fighting?' Mum said contemptuously. 'How disgusting!'

'It was quite common in those days, you know,' Helen said calmly, stirring the chilli. 'You can still see a dip in the field below this house, which was the neighbourhood cockpit. That's where Thomas Quarmby lost all his money. Apparently he kept a brood of fighting cocks in one of your lost outbuildings. But either he had some duds, or someone else just had better ones, for his began to get beaten. And the more they lost, the more money Thomas wagered, until he was cleaned out. So he staked his house on a final battle, and lost that too.'

'Staked his house on a cockfight!' Mum exclaimed. 'He must have been mad. What happened next?'

'He harnessed two horses to his carriage, galloped them up on to the moors, and drove them over a precipice.'

'Oh, no! Was he killed?'

'Well, of course.'

'And the horses?'

'Those too, I suppose. His wife had died a few years earlier, and what became of his children, I don't know.'

'What a horrible story,' said Mum, thoroughly enjoying it.

Very slowly Alastair spooned catfood into a bowl, while Mitt the Kitt wrapped her silky length round his legs. He gave a blurred fraction of attention to Helen's story, but he couldn't concentrate on it, because what had happened to him had been worse, far worse.

He set down the bowl for Mitt the Kitt, and moved

to the sink to wash the spoon. He turned on the tap, and gazed at the running water. All he could see was the staircase leading to the solitary little attic, which Nicola called the Gable Room. He'd never go there again.

When, on Chris's instructions, the ghost-hunters had fanned out into the wax-smelling dimness, he had lost Pete and the twins in the throng. Besides, they were supposed to be going separately. So he'd been on his own when he'd crossed Nicola's bedroom – so safe and ordinary with its posters and teddy-bears – and gone through the further door, on to the dark little landing beyond.

For a moment he'd been tempted to switch on a proper light; but a faint shimmer welled up from the kitchen passage below, and touched the other stairs, which wound on towards the Gable Room. He had begun to climb.

And all at once, he knew that this was the place.

Looking at the running tap, Alastair thought of bonfires, and the way the wind caught the smoke, and sent it billowing over you, till you were gasping and choking. That was how it had been on the Gable Room stairs. He had just reached a narrow window, six steps up, when suddenly something had flooded over him, blinding, smothering. Only it wasn't like bonfire smoke, because it was icy cold, freezing him with its terrifying touch. He had ducked away, and fled, helter-skelter, down two flights of stairs, as if a million ghosts were after him. What a relief to see the line of light under the kitchen door, and to snatch up the cosy, living bundle of Mitt the Kitt!

'There,' said Mum. 'Supper's ready. I'll start calling people in.'

Suddenly the kitchen door flew open – not the one Alastair had used, but another one, leading into the dining-room – and Pete burst through, with a cross look on his face.

'I can't find the Gable Room that Simon and Sukey keep talking about,' he whined. 'They won't tell me where it is. It's not fair. They're always teasing.'

'Oh, dear,' said Mum brightly. 'What a shame. But does it matter?'

'They say there's nothing there, but I want to see all the rooms, and I can't if I don't know the way.'

Mum glanced across the kitchen, and Alastair felt the hair on the back of his neck prickle with dread. He knew what was coming.

'Look, here's Alastair,' said Mum. 'He'll show you.'

'We're – just going to have supper,' Alastair stammered.

'It'll take a while serving everyone, and you won't be long. There are two ways, you see, Peter; up the stairs beyond the door there, or through Nicola's bedroom.'

She went on explaining, while Alastair stood by the sink, rigid. He couldn't go back up, he couldn't.

'It sounds very muddling,' grumbled Pete. 'I don't see why old houses have to be so complicated.'

'Oh, you boys,' said Mum with a laugh. 'Mysterious attics and winding stairs don't mean a thing to you, do they? You like everything modern and scientific. I should think you two would be the last people at the party to find a ghost! Take him up, Alastair, and satisfy his curiosity.' She turned away. 'Goodness, Helen, I'm forgetting the garlic bread.'

There was no escape.

'Come on,' said Alastair.

On a table in the kitchen passage stood two flickering candles. Alastair picked one up, sending their shadows wavering, giant-sized, across the ceiling, while hot wax dripped down his fingers. His hand was shaking.

'You take the candle,' he said.

The first staircase was all right. They emerged on the landing by Nicola's door.

'Up there?' asked Pete.

'Yes.'

The word came out in a sort of squeak. Tentacles of ice seemed to be groping towards him.

'Shall I go first?' Pete volunteered.

Alastair nearly said yes. He could let Pete go, hang back, make some excuse for staying on the landing. After all, there was nothing at the top but the Gable Room, with its sloping ceiling and bare floor. Pete only needed to see it, and come straight down.

Then, all at once, Alastair knew that if he chickened out, and let the fear win, it would get worse. It would master him completely. He would be lost, scared to move round his own home. *And there isn't really anything on the staircase*, his old, scientific self observed. *How can there be?*

'I'll lead!' he gasped, and he pushed past Pete. The candlelight behind him glinted off the narrow window-pane. It dazzled him, bursting into a wave of coldness and panic, which rolled over him drowning him. He shut his eyes, put his head down, and charged.

Then suddenly his feet clattered on the bare floor of the Gable Room. He had survived.

'You're in a hurry,' Pete puffed behind him. 'I suppose you want your supper. Well, there's nothing here. I never believed in ghosts, anyway.'

3

The next day, which was Saturday, Alastair sat down on his bedroom floor with a pile of scientific encyclopedias. They had all helped to tidy up after the party, but now Dad was taking Chris to a football match and Nicola was playing a tape, while Mum relaxed with a cup of coffee. There was a good chance he would be undisturbed.

He needed to solve the mystery of the Gable Room staircase. He liked everything to have a rational explanation, to be clear and definite, and last night's experience could hardly have been more baffling and unaccountable. Yet there must be an explanation. Everything had an explanation.

He thought of beams which triggered automatic doors and security lights. Could there be a similar beam on the staircase, which he had accidentally broken to unloose that terrifying chill? But where was the mechanism, and why had nobody else set it off? For nobody else had. The ghost-hunt had been utterly spookless, as everyone had agreed over the chilli con carne.

All the same, a beam with hidden mechanics and unpredictable working had to be a possibility. Could there be one which responded to his particular chemical make-up, or body temperature? He read the entries on gamma rays and laser beams, and felt blanker than ever.

What about draughts, he wondered. Might a draught, sucked through a hole in the wall or window-frame, create strange currents? He was just sketching a possible diagram, with arrows and spirals of wind – which looked good, but not really convincing – when Louise came in.

'Alastair,' she began, rather plaintively.

'M'm?' He didn't look up.

'I wish you'd play with me.'

'I'm busy.'

The current would depend on windspeed, of course, but it was a windy hillside.

'I've no one to play with,' bleated Louise.

'Try Nicola.'

'She's been doing her nails. She can't move in case she smudges them.'

'Go and find Mitt the Kitt.'

'I want somebody *proper*.'

'Sorry. I've got to work out a scientific problem.'

The size of the hole through which the wind came would be important. Only, if it was just a draught, why hadn't Pete noticed it too?

'Alastair.'

'M'm?'

'Will you help me look for the Bottomless Well?'

'I told you, I'm busy.'

After a while she trailed out again, banging the door.

There was no scientific explanation. But if there was no explanation, what was the explanation of *that*?

Alastair began to feel extremely cross.

He slammed his books shut, and walked to the window. It was a bright, cold, February morning. Sunlight glittered on the frost-whitened ground. Dad's car was bumping away down the lane which ran upwards from the village, past the house. You could see another stretch of it, Alastair remembered, from the Gable Room stairs. It was the lane up which, long ago, Thomas Quarmby had galloped his horses, to kill himself and them.

'Crazy old fool!' Alastair snorted aloud.

He was fed up with Quarmby Hall, its legends and mysteries. It should be tamed, brought into the last decade of the twentieth century.

All at once an idea hit him, bold enough to make him catch his breath. Suppose he took his computer – his most modern possession – into the Gable Room, and fixed it up there? That would show the ghosts what he thought of them. If he could. If he dared.

He opened his door, and looked down the crooked passage towards Nicola's bedroom. The music had stopped, and he thought he could hear her talking to Mum downstairs. Her nails must have dried. He whisked along the passage, across Nicola's bedroom, and opened the door on the far side. There was the tiny landing, with one staircase plunging down to the kitchen, and one winding upwards.

Now, how brave was he feeling?

'Silly old ghost! Beans on toast!' he shouted rapidly into the emptiness.

An affronted chill seemed to descend like rain on to his shoulders. He backed into Nicola's bedroom, and closed the door.

No, he wasn't going to be beaten. He opened the door again. The silence was deathly.

Then he had a second brainwave. He seized Nicola's Walkman, which was lying by her bed, grabbed a tape, and slid the earphones into place. A burst of music sealed him off completely from the eerie quiet.

Now he was in a hurry. With music blaring through his head, he slotted his small folding table under one arm, and a chair under the other, and dashed at the stairs. Clatter, clatter, went his feet, and plinkety-plonk went the protective music in his ears. He reached the top, breathless and unharmed.

His courage mounting, he repeated the process twice, with the keyboard, and then the screen, of his computer. So that was how to beat a nasty something on a tacky old staircase! Thankfully he removed the Walkman, and glanced round the Gable Room. It was dusty and unfurnished, with panelled walls, and a finger of sunlight pointing across the floor.

'Beans on toast!' exclaimed Alastair triumphantly.

He unfolded the table, and set up his computer. Was there a plug socket in this funny little attic? Yes! He bent towards the skirting board – and saw a glint of gold. In the crack between the panelling and the floor, lay a tiny coin, spotlit by the sunshine.

Alastair was on his knees in an instant, trying to poke out the coin. The crack was too narrow for his fingers, but he managed to dislodge it with the sharpened point of his pencil. Out on to the dusty floorboards slid the little golden disc. It must be money, Alastair thought. He picked it up.

'What are you doing?' a voice shrieked.

Alastair sprang to his feet.

Opposite him, across the room, stood a girl he'd never seen before. She was thin and haggard, and an inch or two smaller than him. Her tangled black hair was roughly pushed back from her white face, and her dark eyes blazed so furiously, that he shrank back against the panelling.

'I – found this coin,' he stammered.

'Don't touch it! It's mine!'

And she leaped towards him like a tiger.

With a lightning reflex which surprised even him, Alastair flicked the coin back into the crack. Instantly the girl vanished.

With shaking knees, Alastair sank on to a chair. For several minutes he could only think about his thudding heart and choking breath, and the sweat beading his forehead, then gradually the picture formed in his mind again.

He saw the white-faced girl, with a grubby apron looped up over a dark dress, stretching her arms towards him, and screaming.

But she couldn't reach him because there was a bed in the room, and she was on the far side of it; a black bed, with reddish curtains hanging from the frame overhead.

There was no bed in the room now.

Then he remembered something else. Instead of the February sunshine, the room had been lit only by the pale beam of a candle. It had been standing on a non-existent wooden chest, whose polished lid reflected its tiny flame.

4

'Alastair!'

Mum's voice, calling him from below, restored some sense of normality. Mum could be trusted not to vanish.

Suddenly he couldn't get out of the Gable Room quick enough. He crashed down through the groping chill, and landed in the kitchen, where Mum – yes! completely normal – was talking to the thin-faced Sherlock Holmes man of last night's party.

'Oh, Alastair,' said Mum, 'you remember our guest, Tony Elland? He's got a problem you might be able to help him with.'

'Just my word processor going bananas,' Tony explained. 'I came up to see if your father would know how to sort it out, but I hear you're the whizzkid with hardware.'

Word processors! Alastair wrenched his thoughts away from oak chests and curtained beds, and from a mind-boggling comparison between Nicola's pink face and coloured sweater, and that skinny girl upstairs, all white and black in the candlelight. At least he understood how word processors worked. Mum and the visitor were talking together, and he gathered that they wanted him to go down to Tony's house in the village, and investigate some technical hiccup. He was more than willing to oblige.

He had pulled on his anorak, and was walking down the drive with Tony, before he realized he hadn't said anything to Mum and Nicola about what must be the

Quarmby Hall ghost. Yet how would he begin? 'A funny person appeared when I touched a gold coin'? He felt all minced up with tension.

Tony Elland didn't seem to notice. He was peering about at the hills.

'No, it's quite invisible. That meant security, of course.'

'Sorry. What?' Alastair realized with a jolt he was being spoken to.

'I'm looking out for Whinnerah Clough Farm.'

Did that have a ghost too, Alastair wondered, reverting instantly to his own thoughts. Even if he told his family about the Gable Room, how would they react? He imagined Chris exploding in hoots of laughter, and Nicola staring as if he'd put on odd socks; Dad raising sensible objections, Mum over-eager to believe him, and Louise bursting into frightened tears.

'I guess they didn't often come down here,' Tony was saying.

'No,' Alastair replied automatically.

'Yellow traders kept out of the public eye.'

'M'm,' agreed Alastair. He'd no idea what Tony was talking about.

Round a bend in the lane they saw the village beneath them, like a sagging clothes-line, strung between twin props of the church and a disused railway station, blinking through weather-torn firs.

'There's my cottage,' said Tony, 'just past the pub. That little one.'

Most things in the village were small. The Fleece itself looked low and humble, though trying to inflate its own importance with wintry window-boxes and bleak, outdoor tables.

'The beer's good,' Tony remarked.

'Yes. Dad says so.'

If anything in life was for real, it was Dad enjoying his pint, and buying crisps all round.

No, the word processor was real too. It stood in the window of Tony's cottage, which they entered from the back, through a door divided like a stable door.

'It's seized up somehow,' Tony explained, gesturing in the direction of the word processor. 'It's refusing to co-operate. I've tried hitting it and swearing at it, but it's probably my fault. I'm hopeless with machines.'

Alastair eyed it, assessing its functions. It looked comfortably straightforward after his conundrums with laser beams and draughts – let alone ghosts! – but everything was out of joint today, and it was safest to consult the manual, which lay beside it on the table. He picked it up, and the nice, flexible book, with its clear diagrams, was immensely reassuring. At the mere touch, he felt his stunned brain clicking back into normal gear.

'I've done an article, a spin-off from the book I'm writing. I wanted to get it out to a few magazine editors.'

Once again, Alastair wasn't listening to Tony. He flipped through the pages, mastering the data, in control again.

'Have you tried this key here? D'you see?'

And, like his brain, the word processor unscrambled itself. It sprang into revitalized action, churning out printed sheets.

'Marvellous! You've cracked it,' Tony exclaimed.

'That's all right,' said Alastair. 'It was easy.'

'You can call it easy.' Tony shook his head admiringly.

Out shot the pages, and a heavy black title caught Alastair's eye. *The Yellow Traders of Whinnerah Clough.* Hadn't they been mentioned at the party, as well as on the way down to the village? Soothed by success, Alastair felt calm enough to inquire.

'What are yellow traders?' he asked.

23

'Coiners,' said Tony.

Like that – whatever it was – on the stairs, the answer froze Alastair's blood. In his mind's eye, he saw the piece of gold in the Gable Room.

'What are coiners?'

'They were people who forged gold coins, back in the 1760s. They clipped the edges off gold guineas – and guineas were valuable coins, worth more than a pound. You could buy a lot with a guinea. The yellow traders saved the clippings, melted them down, and made new coins for themselves, and then they put the clipped gold back into ordinary circulation.'

So the treacherous word processor was pointing him straight back to the Gable Room! Out flew another sheet. *The Yellow Traders of Whinnerah Clough.*

'Couldn't people tell if their coins were funny?' Alastair asked.

'Not very easily,' said Tony. 'You see, at that time the Royal Mint was terribly slack about producing currency. New coins were very scarce, so a lot of the old ones were practically worn away with hard usage. Which meant that faked or clipped coins could pass muster, especially when most people were fairly ignorant and unsophisticated, and not much used to handling money.'

'And you got them round here?' said Alastair.

'Yes, quite a lot. There was this coining gang, which operated from Whinnerah Clough Farm. The landlord of the Fleece, who seems to have been in the gang too, passed over guineas for them to clip, and then foisted the clipped gold back on to his customers, while the coiners spent the fakes they had made on themselves.'

He explained how the once busy village road, with its eighteenth century traffic of wagons and packhorses, had provided an easy supply of ready money for an unscrupulous landlord; but Alastair had another question, perhaps the most important of all.

'How could you tell if a coin had been clipped?'

'Officials went round with little scales to weigh them. And if they were too light – '

'No. I mean nowadays.'

'Oh, I see. Well, a George II guinea should be twenty-five millimetres across, so if it was clipped, it would be slightly smaller. But there aren't any still in existence.'

Alastair wondered. He could, if he was brave enough, take a ruler up to the Gable Room when he got home, and check. For it seemed to him that there might still be a few around which Tony didn't know about.

Only, would that witchy girl spring out?

At least, if she did, he would be better prepared.

'And they called it the yellow trade,' Tony was saying, 'because of gold being yellow. Sort of, anyway. Besides, it was a convenient cover-up, to use a term most people didn't understand, because coining could be very danger-ous.'

'How d'you mean?' asked Alastair, surprised.

'If coiners were caught, they were usually executed. Hanged by the neck, until they were dead. Well, that's all the copies I need. I'm really grateful for your help.'

5

Why am I doing this? Alastair asked himself.

When he'd got back to Quarmby Hall, he'd found that some of Nicola's friends had arrived; a whole chattering of them. (Brilliant! He'd invented a new collective noun.) Mum was cutting cake for them and Louise was hanging around, so he'd gone straight upstairs, intent on the experiment he'd planned as he walked home. He got out a ruler – and panic hit him.

Why am I doing this?

He forced himself to pause and answer the question.

I'm going to fish out that coin in the Gable Room. I want to measure it, not because it matters to me to find something rare, but because, if there is something wrong with it, it might partly explain why everything in the room went funny, and that girl – that ghost? – appeared. It's perfectly easy. I shall just put the ruler against the coin, and stay calm even if she pounces out again.

Ruler in hand, he made his way to Nicola's bedroom, and stopped in dismay. The Walkman was still in the Gable Room. He'd have to face the staircase without it.

Think of the first men going into space, he told himself, or divers, plumbing uncharted waters. Compared with risks like those, what were a few stairs? Taking them at a pounding rush, he reached the Gable Room. The chill never actually harmed him. He was almost getting used to it.

His computer was still there, and the Walkman. With the tip of his ruler, he flicked the gold coin out of its crevice, and picked it up.

Instantly he was back in the ancient bedroom, with the white-faced girl screaming at him across the bed. Prepared though he was, his heart lurched inside his chest.

'What are you doing?' she shrieked, as she had before.

'Just – er –' he faltered. And then, with an unexpected rush of pity, he saw the thinness of the little hands stretched towards him, and how reddened and sore-looking they were, with dirty, broken nails; unloved hands.

'It's all right,' he heard himself saying. 'Don't worry. I shan't hurt you. I'm your friend.'

'You're stealing my money.'

'I'm not. Look, you can take it.'

He held out the coin, and she snatched it with trembling haste. She was scared, he realized, even more scared than he was. Her fury covered swirling depths of panic.

'Go away!' she ordered, clutching the gold. 'Go away!'

But how could he? The door was shut, enclosing him in a different Quarmby Hall from the one he knew. Instead of the computer on its table, the oak chest now stood by the wall. Until the coin was restored to its hiding place, he couldn't get away. Not properly, not to his own world and time.

Oddly enough, the thought steadied him. He felt that, at last, he was beginning to understand what was happening. He had changed time zones with the coin, and to escape, he would need to get it back.

The first step was to put her at her ease. He moved a little way round the bed, smiling.

'You've no need to be afraid of me,' he said. 'I'm just an ordinary person. I'm called Alastair Croft. Who are you?'

She stared at him, bewilderment in her dark eyes, but she too was calmer now.

'Don't you know? Haven't they told you?'

'Are you – a Quarmby?' he guessed.

The sigh she gave was the saddest sound he'd ever heard.

'Aye,' she said. 'I'm a Quarmby. Or I was, once. I'm Martha, Martha Jane Quarmby. But I don't know as how you could tell. I don't look like a Quarmby no more. I look like what they've made me – Mrs Gledhill's kitchenmaid.'

There was so much information in her answer, that Alastair needed to pause and think it through. This desolate, fragile girl belonged to the old family from the Hall, yet somehow she'd lost her status and her freedom, and been turned into a servant. Had she lost them because her father had lost the house?

'Are you Thomas Quarmby's daughter?' he ventured.

She gulped, as if she was going to answer, and then great, round tears began running down her face, and splashing onto her ugly black dress.

'I'm sorry!' exclaimed Alastair, stricken. 'I shouldn't have asked.'

'It don't matter. Everyone knows. Not that they care.'

'They *must* care.'

'Not them. Not Mr Gledhill, as is master here now, nor Mrs Gledhill, so puffed up and proud that her husband owns the biggest house in these parts. And all because he got his hands on two fine Spanish fighting cocks before Father had a chance. Mr Gledhill were nowt then, nowt but a petty lawyer, wanting to be somebody.' She dashed away her tears, fixing despairing eyes on Alastair again. 'That night, when Mr Gledhill's Spanish cocks had bested Father's, I were alone down yonder by the window. I heard the horses galloping, and the whip cracking. My father drove up by the moor as if the Gytrash were after him. I felt so cold, you see, as cold as death, to hear those flying hooves as they went past the house, and away. I knew I'd not see my father again.'

She shivered like a leaf, and Alastair tugged the thin quilt off the bed to wrap round her. She looked at him in astonishment.

'You're kind – like James,' she began, and sobs choked her.

'Who's James?'

'He's my brother. I've no one left, only him.'

'Will he be coming up here soon?'

'Nay.' She sounded surprised. 'Mr Gledhill don't let him into Owlsnap no more. He can't so much as step over the threshold.'

Owlsnap? a corner of Alastair's brain queried, but Martha's words ran on.

'He's been the potboy down at the Fleece since Father died; James Quarmby, as should be owner of Owlsnap and all its lands, instead of Mr Gledhill.'

Owlsnap. Owl Snape. Alastair made the connection, joining Martha's words like jigsaw puzzle pieces. But even as he put them together, his heart was unaccountably sinking. No, not unaccountably. Martha's brother worked at the Fleece, whose landlord helped the yellow traders. And the little gold coin, which did such odd things, which Martha was clutching now in her bone-cold hand, suggested sickeningly that she could be involved with the gang as well. And that was appallingly dangerous, as Tony had pointed out.

He put his arm round her shoulders, and she snuggled against him like a stray cat.

'Can't you get away from here, you and James?' he asked.

'Oh, if we could!' she cried. 'Over the hills and far away, with Owlsnap left behind for ever. But how can we? Where'd we go?'

Alastair didn't know. He hugged her tightly, hoping his warmth might thaw her frozen body.

'What makes you so good to me?' she asked wonderingly; and then she gave a great yawn. 'Eh, I'm tired! I were up at daybreak, and now it must be nigh on midnight.'

She eased herself away, and dropped on to the bed. Through her tangled hair she peeped at him.

'Who are you, then?' she asked, as if she'd forgotten.

'Alastair Croft. I'm staying in the house. Look, if you're going to sleep, you'd better be properly covered. I'll pull the blanket over you. How's that?'

'Lovely,' she murmured, and fell headlong into exhausted sleep. The coin dropped from her hand, and ran spinning across the floor. Alastair picked it up, and looked at it.

On one side was a blurred coat of arms; on the other, a bewigged and sneering king. Round the uneven edge ran smudged and mutilated letters, but whether hard usage or clipping had damaged it, Alastair couldn't tell.

Now was the moment to measure it – but no! The ruler, together with the computer and the Walkman, were separated from him by nearly two hundred and thirty years.

Suddenly the Gable Room felt like a trap; only it was a trap he could free himself from. He flew to the crack under the panelling, pushed in the coin – and there were the nice modern things, just where he'd left them!

Measuring the coin was a problem he could forget for the moment. He'd had enough adventures for one morning. It was still morning. A glance at his watch in the frosty sunshine assured him of that. He collected the ruler and Walkman, and headed for the stairs.

It was funny that he didn't mind the chill this time. He even lingered for a moment, thinking of poor Martha, frozen in horror by the window, while her father galloped up the lane to his death.

6

For the next few days Alastair wandered about in a daze. He forgot things, he dropped things, he didn't answer when people spoke to him.

'Supersonic brain disease,' suggested Chris at the supper table.

The roar of family laughter jerked Alastair back to reality.

'What's that?'

'We're alarmed by the speed at which your brain's crumbling,' said Chris.

'It's not crumbling,' Alastair retorted.

'Well, maybe it's your ears then.'

'What Chris means,' explained Mum kindly, 'is that Nicola was asking for your help, and you didn't seem to hear.'

'Sorry. What d'you want help with?'

'Maths homework,' said Nicola. 'I'm stuck, and you're tons better at Maths than Chris.'

'So that's put his nose out of joint,' remarked Louise.

'Shut up, Lou!' Chris ordered.

Splinters of argument launched across the table distracted everyone's attention, and left Alastair free to wonder whether Martha and James had ever quarrelled in the days when they were prosperous and happy.

Martha was haunting Alastair in a different way now. He couldn't get her out of his mind. As Nicola's smooth, pink-tipped fingers reached for the peppermill, his thoughts flew to Martha's work-reddened hands; and

32

Martha's dark tangle of hair superimposed itself over Louise's neat, blonde bob.

The Quarmbys wouldn't have sat in the kitchen, of course. They'd have used one of the little panelled parlours which had lost their identity in Dad's big sitting-room. And maybe they hadn't been happy at all. Maybe they'd sat shivering, with nothing – no music, no computer games, no videos, possibly even no books – to divert their anxious thoughts from what their father might be wagering, in the cockpit below the house, against the fine Spanish cocks of lawyer Gledhill.

It was because he felt so involved with Martha, so oddly protective, that he'd never mentioned her to the family. Their disbelieving reactions would have been like clumsy boots trampling through a spider's web.

Besides, if he'd told them, they'd have wanted proof, and what proof was there? At different times they'd all been up to the Gable Room, and none of them had sensed the chill of Martha's despair. Probably they'd fail to see the coin, or it wouldn't work for them.

Once, Alastair had thought that everything in the natural world could be proved in a straightforward way, but clearly there were grey areas beyond the borders of science, psychic regions where the normal rules of time and space didn't apply. And he, the scientist, had strayed – maddeningly, thrillingly – into one of them, simply by picking up an ancient guinea. He'd be bending spoons next!

But there were still things that could be proved; whether the coin was the right size, for example.

'He's gone off into a dream again. He must be in love,' teased Mum – but kindly.

'Love! Alastair!' Chris guffawed loudly.

'Mum's just being romantic again,' said Nicola. 'Can you come to my room now, Alastair? Tracey's going to ring at half past.'

'Hang on for a couple of minutes,' said Alastair, and ran upstairs to his own room.

It took about five, in fact. With compasses, he drew a circle twenty-five millimetres in diameter on a piece of card. He snipped it out, rolled back his sleeve, blu-tacked the circle onto his forearm, outlined it in black biro, ripped it off, and pulled down his sleeve.

'Coming!' he called to Nicola.

He didn't see why marks on his skin should disappear, given that his skin had to go back with him into the past.

It was never any good trying to explain Maths to Nicola. 'I haven't that sort of brain,' she'd say. All she wanted was for him to complete a page of problems, which he did as quickly as possible, while she leafed through a magazine, and smeared stuff from a tube over a spot on her chin.

'There's the phone. It'll be Tracey,' she said. 'We're doing our French together. Thanks, Alastair. I'll copy it later.'

She grabbed a pen and a few books from her bag, and rushed away as Mum called upstairs to her.

Alastair was left alone. He glanced at the second door, wondering.

There were two problems to solve – and they had nothing to do with Maths! One was whether the coin had been clipped. The other was whether Martha was involved with the yellow traders. Or Martha and James together. If they were, and he went back into Martha's world, he could find himself in the middle of a very nasty situation.

Mr Rogers, a teacher at school, had been talking about capital punishment that very day, all lightly and cheer-fully, because it had been given up long ago, like slavery and boy sweeps climbing up inside chimneys. Some of the class egged him on, demanding gory details, excited to hear that, two hundred years ago, children of their own age could have been executed.

And Alastair thought of Martha . . .

If he went back, he might be able to work out a way of helping her. He could ask her straight out if she knew the people at Whinnerah Clough Farm, and warn her how dangerous it might be to associate with them.

Or, even better, he would ask her to put him in touch with James. James might well be the link between Martha and the yellow traders, and talking to a boy of around his own age could be easier. He would give the warning to James, and tell him not to entangle Martha in such life-threatening perils.

There was no need to bother about the Walkman. He could cope with the icy stairs now. He whisked up, scratched out the coin from its hiding place, and saw normality dissolve into the gloom of the past.

Martha lay on the bed, huddled beneath the quilt. The uncurtained window showed a grey sky. It was earlier than last time, six or seven o'clock, perhaps.

She stirred as he approached, half waking, and raising her head.

'Is that James?' she asked eagerly.

'No, it's me, Alastair Croft. D'you remember me?'

'Oh.' She seemed partly to remember, partly to lose interest, dropping back on to her pillow. She'd gone to sleep in her black frock and grubby apron, as if she had no proper nightdress, though something which might have been a crumpled nightcap half covered the tangle of her hair.

'Aren't you pleased to see me again?' Alastair asked.

She gave her head a little, indifferent shake.

'I thought you was James – but he only comes in

35

dreams,' she said sadly, and closed her eyes.

At least that gave him a chance to test the coin. He pushed up his sleeve, discovered with relief that the inked ring was still there, and laid the coin in the middle. It was much too small! A pale rim ran between it and the twenty-five millimetre circle.

So it was clipped gold, it really was!

Although he had been expecting it, he felt cold with dismay. He liked Martha, and her frail defencelessness didn't seem to tie up with crime at all. But why had she hidden the coin, unless she felt guilty about it?

He dropped it into his pocket. It was his means of escape, so he had to be careful with it. Then he moved to the bed.

'Martha.'

She opened tired eyes, blinking up at him.

'Can you tell me how to find James? Is he at the Fleece?'

She sat bolt upright, looking frightened.

'Why d'you want him?'

'To talk to him.'

'What'll you be talking on?'

He couldn't say, 'the yellow trade'. He just couldn't.

'I want to get to know him, like I've got to know you.'

'People don't want to know us,' Martha replied bitterly, 'disgraced and disinherited as we be. We're not like Quarmbys no more, not like the Quarmbys were, time out of mind.'

'Can't something be done about it?' exclaimed Alastair, side-tracked by the rush of pity which swept over him.

'There's naught to be done. James vows he'll buy Owl-snap back one day. He's bent on it. I've told him he's mad, but he won't listen. He never could do it, Alastair.

He'd need – nay, I can't tell how many guineas.'

What were a potboy's wages for pulling pints and washing mugs? Not much more than pennies, probably.

'Did James earn the gold you hid under the skirting board?' Alastair ventured.

'Why d'you ask?' she cried, her voice shrill with alarm. 'You never ought to have touched it. Oh, God! It's not there! Where is it?'

'I've got it here. It's quite safe. I'm not stealing it. I just wondered if James gave it to you to save, as a sort of first instalment to buying Owlsnap back.'

She didn't answer, but dropped her eyes, knotting the corner of the quilt round her fingers. Her silence seemed to prove that his guess had been right. Alastair wished he'd never come back. How could he cope with the terror, and evil, and tragedy, which seemed to swirl through the room?

Then Martha looked up.

'If you're bound for the Fleece, will you happen take me?'

Alastair hadn't expected that. He hesitated.

'Please,' begged Martha, and he realized that he could resist her no more than he could resist Mitt the Kitt when she wound herself round his legs, and mewed for food.

'All right,' he said. 'Let's go.'

7

Grey twilight gleamed through the window onto the staircase. Martha crept down first, wrapped in a shawl. Alastair tiptoed after her. He was wondering what the rest of the house would be like, and vaguely expecting jolly gentlemen with punchbowls, blazing fires, and beribboned maids carrying steaming pies, like he'd seen on Christmas cards or jigsaw puzzles.

But of course it wasn't like that. It was cold; cold with the piercing chill of stone floors and stone walls, two hundred years before central heating. And though a wan light glimmered on a ledge, it only made the kitchen passage blacker. There were no jolly voices, no savoury whiffs of pie or punch, just ancient, shivery darkness hemming him in.

'Take this,' whispered Martha.

'What?' He couldn't see.

'George Brunton's cloak. He'll not be needing it tonight.'

She thrust an armful of thick cloth at him. Its reek of horses told him that George Brunton must be a groom.

'I'll be warm enough,' he protested.

'Don't you be daft. Put it on. It'll cover – Ssh!'

A door crashed open, the kitchen door of modern Quarmby Hall, and – yes – it was Owlsnap's kitchen too. Where the Aga now stood, there was a stone fireplace, with a huge black kettle slung on an iron bar above smouldering embers. A mess of dirty pots and spoons littered the table, while the stink of smoke mingled with cabbage and burnt fat billowed out.

'And if I've more trouble from thee,' a voice screamed, 'thou'll find thisen in bed wi' no supper, same as yon little madam in t'attic.'

A tiny figure, like a frightened mouse, scurried past Alastair, and vanished into the old larder where Dad's filing cabinets lived.

'Shut t'door, thou varmint!'

A vast, aproned shape burst from the shadows of the kitchen, to slam the door with a resounding bang.

'Now!' hissed Martha, and they whisked out through the back porch into the February evening. Alastair paused in astonishment. Behind Quarmby Hall, as he knew it, stretched a wild garden, its emptiness over-grown with bushes and brambles; but here, stables, barns and pigsties jostled almost to the kitchen wall.

'Come on. Mind the well!'

Martha flew off, and he plunged after her, through a maze of lost buildings, and out into the lane, which was, thankfully, still recognizable, though rough and pitted without its tarmac surface.

'What was that about going to bed without supper?' asked Alastair, once they were clear of the house. He hadn't liked the threat.

'It's how we're punished. Me or Jacky catch it most days; him from Cook, me from Mrs Gledhill.'

'Was that Jacky running away?'

'Aye. He's the turnspit. He'll have been in trouble, like me.'

'What had you done?'

'Dropped a plate; china, it were, not wood nor pewter. So it broke.'

'Is that all?'

'It's enough,' she said, 'when you're a Quarmby, and Mrs Gledhill's the mistress.'

'How awful!' said Alastair, appalled.

'Why d'you talk so strange?' she asked abruptly.

It was the first sign she'd noticed anything different about him. Funnily enough, people at school commented on the same thing.

'I don't come from Yorkshire,' he explained. 'I was born near London.'

'Are they London clothes – yon queer breeches and woollen shirt?'

'Yes,' he answered, just managing not to laugh, for she meant his jeans and sweater.

'Nay, folks must look fair outlandish,' Martha marvelled.

By now they had reached the village. The muddy lane wound between dark cottages, shuttered for the night. Alastair stumbled over a stone, and put his foot in a puddle. How awful to live before street lighting!

Then, round a corner, he saw a splash of yellow. The Fleece's uncurtained windows shone through the darkness.

'Not the front door,' whispered Martha. 'We'll go to the back.'

'Why?'

'So we can see what James is at. And I don't like the landlord.'

She turned under an archway into a yard lit by lanterns.

Alastair stared, amazed. He'd seen behind the Fleece when he went to Tony Elland's house, and there was nothing but a small, drab car-park. Now stables, with that inescapable horsy smell, enclosed a large square. Long noses poked over divided doors – like the one in Tony's cottage, he realized – and more ponies were tethered in the yard, nuzzling into piles of hay. The bundles with which they had been loaded were stacked in heaps.

40

'There must be a packhorse train, crossing into Lancashire. I wish I could go too,' sighed Martha.

Stablemen were hurrying everywhere with buckets and pitchforks. Martha edged past, and through a little door at the back of the inn. Shadowy stairs rose beyond.

'This way,' she murmured.

Alastair followed her up, and they emerged into a little railed gallery high above the bar parlour. He looked down into a crowded room.

It was hazed and blurred by tobacco fumes, and spiralling candle smoke. The candles, burning on the bar counter and the long tables, threw their flickering light over tight huddles of men, clustered round bottles and tankards. Here and there, a face, lined and haggard, showed pale in the gloom, and firelight touched a patched coat on stooping shoulders, or the brim of a battered hat.

'Yon's James,' muttered Martha, pointing.

He was standing behind the bar; a boy who looked like Chris in age, but unlike him in every other way. James's face was colourless, pointed and hollow-cheeked; and his hair fell in dark, dishevelled elflocks on to his collar. Perhaps it had once been tied back, for a ribbon dangled untidily from a single strand; but everything about James was untidy, from his smudged hands to his untucked shirt. Plainly, he didn't care. He was twisting a cloth round and round inside a pewter mug, and gazing into the fire with dark, faraway eyes.

'A potboy,' sighed Martha. 'Him as should be master of Owlsnap, and all the lands around.'

'He doesn't seem to mind,' observed Alastair.

'He feeds on dreams,' said Martha. 'Daft ones, but they keep him happy.'

'Dreams of buying back Owlsnap?'

'Aye.'

How stupid could you get, thought Alastair, how downright crazy, spaced out, and drugged by fantasy? He pictured Owlsnap's crooked, looming bulk, and then he looked back at the slight, unkempt boy with the dish-cloth. James would never manage it.

Unless – Alastair remembered the hidden coin, now in his pocket. A dishonest coin, he suspected, from a dishonest, gold-clipping gang. That coin seemed the key to everything.

'How did James get the guinea you were keeping for him?' he asked Martha sharply.

'The landlord, Mr Pearson, gave it him. It were pay-ment for an errand James did.'

'A *guinea*? For an *errand*?'

'Well – I don't rightly know – 'Martha was suddenly flustered.

Dim as it was, he could see her cheeks reddening, and her eyes flinched away from his.

'Some errand!' said Alastair grimly. 'I'm going down to talk to James.'

But before he could move, the door from the street below was flung open, and a tall man in a long-skirted coat pushed his way into the room.

8

The newcomer strode forward, and plonked down a square box on the bar counter.

'Landlord!' he shouted.

There was silence in the room. Hands, grasping mugs, were still, but heads swivelled towards the corner where the landlord was serving a customer. Alastair saw him spin round; a bald little man with pixie ears.

'Good evening, sir,' he answered briskly. 'James, serve the gentleman.'

James blinked, dropped the dishcloth, and laid his hand abstractedly on a beer barrel, but the newcomer shook his head.

'I'm not here to drink,' he said. 'I've important business to transact. I'm an exciseman in His Majesty's service, landlord, and I've come to examine the coins you have at this inn.'

A swoop, thought Alastair, like a police raid. The real thing! And he felt, not excited, as he would have expected, but rigid with alarm, both for Martha who was biting the corner of her apron in terror, and James who still stood dreamily with his hand on the barrel. He was aware, too, of tension in the room below, of alert faces watching the landlord.

The little man was looking puzzled.

'What makes you question my coinage, sir?' he demanded.

'The magistrates have heard reports of mutilated guineas circulating in these parts. To be precise, sir,

43

clipped gold.'

'Bless my soul!' exclaimed the landlord. 'They must be mistaken. I never heard tell of such a thing. Anyone here know aught about it?'

He threw a bold, challenging stare around the room. He was looking for support, Alastair guessed, but it didn't come. There were uncertain mutterings, dark looks were exchanged, and a man by the fire spoke up.

'I carried a clipped guinea into Lancashire last week. It was palmed off on me somewhere, though how and when I can't tell. I had to chuck it away, and pay for my lodging with another.'

'That was wrong,' said the exciseman severely. 'You should have taken it to a magistrate. It might have been used as evidence. I've authority to test all the guineas in these parts, and anyone possessed of faked or clipped coins will be punished without mercy. So, landlord, bring out your guineas.'

Alastair found himself gripping the gallery railings.

'You're wasting your time,' sneered the landlord. 'But, if you insist – '

And, with a little skip and a twirl, he was behind the bar, pushing James out of the way, and flinging open a nest of drawers under the counter. He scooped out a few handfuls of coins, separated gold from copper, and tossed the guineas down in front of the exciseman.

'Try this!' he cried, as they chinked and rattled. 'And this, and this! I dare swear you'll find them all sound.'

'We'll see,' replied the exciseman.

He took from his box a small weighing scale, with two swinging pans, and began to balance the guineas, one by one, against a counterpoise. Each time the pans swung level. A taut, watchful silence filled the room. Some of the customers, at least, had their doubts, while others were only curious.

44

'Is that all?' asked the exciseman, when the last coin had been tested.

'All?' shrieked the landlord indignantly. 'How many more do you expect? Use your eyes. This is a poor house, in a poor village.'

'Don't play the innocent,' retorted the exciseman. 'Many rich travellers use this road, as well you know.'

'What do you mean? Do you accuse me of lying? Of hiding money away from you? There are my empty drawers. What more do you want?'

The little landlord was jumping up and down in a frenzy of indignation, but the exciseman remained stolid and calm.

'Have any of your customers got coins they're uncertain of?'

His eyes swept the room. One or two of the drinkers pulled out a coin, but the scales proved nothing wrong.

'Ah, well.' The exciseman suddenly relaxed and smiled. 'I was mistaken, it seems. Tales get about. Some fellow mentioned the Fleece, but he was clearly in error. Here's a guinea of my own, landlord, and you may pour me a tot of rum, to warm me for my ride home.'

'I'll brew you a toddy, sir.' The landlord was suddenly in excellent spirits too. 'A rum toddy, as hot as hell and as strong as death. There's a kettle on the fire, you see, and spices and lemons behind the bar. A *lemon*, James, as quick as you can. Here's how we make our celebrated toddy at the Fleece, sir.'

With a bow and a flourish, the landlord set out his ingredients on a fireside table, between the exciseman, and the man who'd taken the clipped guinea into Lancashire.

'Any gentleman care for a glass – on the house?' he invited, and several more customers pulled up their chairs.

Alastair watched, fascinated, as the landlord rasped sugar from a misshapen lump, squeezed his lemon, and sprinkled spices carefully into a punchbowl. Dad made punch like that sometimes at Christmas. He glanced at Martha, hoping she was enjoying the performance too – and saw her eyes, wide with alarm, still fixed on her brother.

Quietly, James had shifted a barrel out of a corner behind the bar where it stood. Quietly, with a knifeblade, he prised up the edge of a floorboard, removed something bulky, slid it into a capacious pocket, and pushed the barrel back into place. Quietly, he stole away through a side door.

For a moment Alastair stared at James's purposeful movements with astonishment. Then he realized what they meant.

'Quick!' he whispered to Martha. 'We must stop him.'

'Oh . . .' She hesitated, stiff with dismay at what they had seen.

'Yes. Now! Come on.'

He grabbed her arm, pulling her after him down the steep stairs. The heavy cloak flapped and swirled, catching his legs, so that he stumbled, and hurtled out into the yard, crashing against a stableman with a bucket of water. Both of them went flying. Alastair landed in a haypile amongst the prancing legs of a startled pony, while the stableman swore, and the bucket thumped away over the cobbles.

He scrambled to his feet, still hampered by folds of now damp cloth.

'You – !'

But the stableman's accent was so thick, Alastair couldn't catch his words. He lunged at Alastair, and Alastair jumped back, cracking his elbow painfully against the wall.

46

'Oh, Alastair!'

And, with Martha's agonized voice, he heard the skittering hoofbeats of a pony kicked to a trot from a standstill. He saw her, halfway across the yard, and raced towards her.

'That was James,' she said.

The hoofbeats died away along the road.

'He's going to Whinnerah Clough, I suppose,' said Alastair, rubbing his elbow.

Martha gave a little cry.

'How come you know?'

'I'd guessed he was involved with the yellow traders before we came to the Fleece. When I saw him scrabbling under that barrel, I was certain. The landlord must have a hidden cache of guineas, which James takes to be clipped.'

The despairing way Martha buried her face in her hands, and shook with noiseless sobs, proved that he was right.

'Come on,' said Alastair. 'We can't catch up with James when he's riding. We might as well get back to Owlsnap.'

And he set off along the dark, rutted lane, with Martha like a quivering shadow beside him. He felt bruised and battered by his fall, and strangely upset by the plight of Martha and James.

'The landlord's clever,' he remarked presently. 'He distracted the exciseman, and everyone else, with his toddy, so that the coast was clear for James to slip away. I wonder if 'lemon' was a code word?'

'What shall you do?' wept Martha, between chattering teeth. 'You'll not tell on him to Mr Gledhill, will you?'

'No,' said Alastair. The promise was easy enough. After the evening's events, the idea of meddling still further with the inhabitants of long ago Owlsnap was appalling. But all the same, what *should* he do? Leave

47

Martha's brother to rush headlong to the gallows? A little sketched figure from a game of Hangman danced before his eyes in the darkness. He swallowed, feeling sick.

'James doesn't know what he's at,' sobbed Martha. 'He's fair mazed with his troubles. He'd never have given me the clipped guinea if he'd knowed it was wrong, or perilous.'

'So you knew it was clipped!' Alastair exclaimed. 'I thought you must have done.'

'That's why I hid it. I were so frightened. Oh, but Alastair,' she put her hand on his arm beseechingly, 'if you only understood how good James is, how kind.'

Or how crazy, thought Alastair. But he didn't say anything, only reached for Martha's thin fingers, and squeezed them.

'He must be stopped,' she said despairingly. 'Can you help?'

9

But nothing was settled when they got back to the Gable Room. Alastair felt exhausted, his usually clear, crisp mind as cloaked and muffled as his body was. He didn't see how he could respond to Martha's appeal. What could he do to help her and James, in the confusing, frightening world of the past? He made a few vague promises, pushed the coin under the skirting board, and thankfully restored himself and his surroundings to normality.

It was marvellous to run down to Nicola's warm, well-lit room, to the cosiness of teddy-bears and posters. But how tired he was! He flopped on to the bed, and closed his eyes.

'What on *earth* are you doing?'

Nicola bounced in, bright and healthy in her clean, trendy track-suit.

'Sorry. I felt sleepy.'

'You don't have to drop off on my bed. You've a perfectly good one of your own. Where's my mag? There's a freebie Tracey's interested in – soft moulding hair wax. It could be worth a try.'

When Tracey and Nicola had shining, immaculate hair already? When freebies were about as essential to them as ice-cream on Christmas cake?

Nicola picked up her magazine.

'Just move yourself, will you,' she ordered. 'I don't want your ponging socks all over my duvet.'

And she whisked back to the phone.

Ponging *socks*! If she'd been wearing George Brunton's cloak all evening, she'd know what a pong really was.

But of course it hadn't been all evening. He glanced at the bedside clock, and saw that only five twentieth-century minutes had passed since he'd finished Nicola's Maths. He still had most of the evening to get through.

This could have been a moment for playing one of his computer games – if the computer hadn't been in the Gable Room. Or he could have invented his own game; something about gold coins, and whether you could clip one before an exciseman zapped you. Or whether you could zap a coiner before he'd finished clipping a guinea, which might be a better way round. He could call the game 'The Yellow Trade', send in details to a computer games' magazine, market it even . . .

But no. The yellow trade wasn't a game, and the yellow traders at Whinnerah Clough weren't comic, cartoon characters. Into his imagination sprang a picture of a dim, smoky room, rather like the bar at the Fleece, where lean, shaggy-haired men sweated over their shears besides a furnace, and all was black, and evil, and horrible. And into it wandered James, like a sheep into a wolves' den.

Alastair gave a start.

Because that, probably, was exactly what had happened. And when the wolfish coiners were sent to the gallows, they might well have dragged James with them, and Martha's heart would have been broken. The storybook phrase could have been for real, thought Alastair, flinching as his busy imagination now threw up a picture of Martha pining with sorrow, all alone in the Gable Room.

He couldn't cope with his whirling thoughts any longer. He jumped off the bed, and hurried down to the security of the big sitting-room.

The fire crackled, the television mumured soothingly, there was a fragrance of coffee, and a savoury tang from a bowl of salt and vinegar crisps. Nicola must have finished her phone call, for everyone was in the room. Dad had recently put up some shelves, nice dark ones, marked like eyebrows against the pinky-apricot wall, and Mum was fishing out ornaments and other bits and pieces from a still-unpacked box, choosing which to display. Louise was helping her, Dad and Chris were playing chess, while Nicola was scribbling her application for the soft moulding hair wax.

They showed no surprise, no special interest, when he appeared. They didn't know he'd visited another century since they last saw him. As far as they knew, he'd only been lolling upstairs for a minute of two. Lolling! Just what he needed. He crashed into a deep, comfortable chair, and let every muscle sag.

'Who's this?' Louise was asking.

She held up a miniature portrait in a gold frame.

'That's my grandmother,' said Mum. 'The Scottish one. I'd like to have her on the shelf.'

And she placed the picture beside the other small objects she'd chosen.

'Was she nice?' inquired Louise.

'She was a bit strange. She had second sight, which is always odd.'

'What does second sight mean?'

Mum considered.

'It means being able to see through layers of time, and knowing what has happened in the past, and what's to come in the future. Exciting, but weird. It's supposed to run in families, but luckily none of us has inherited it.'

'Seeing through layers of time!' exclaimed Chris. 'What a crazy idea. Nobody could.'

His scorn infuriated Alastair.

'It's not crazy,' he retorted. 'It could happen.'

'Like how?'

'I can't explain. I just know it could happen. I *know*.'

Rising irresistibly inside him was a burning need to prove – not so much to Chris as to the cool, scientific person he'd been himself, before he came to Quarmby Hall – that it was possible to move through time, and experience strange fragments of the past. They were only fragments, as tantalizing as the torn pages of a book. But once they'd been reality. Once, a boy not much older than himself, had heedlessly drifted into terrible danger. He saw again that nightmare picture of James, dangling from a rope like a pin man in a paper game, and his heart thumped violently.

'Hey, you've gone all pale, Alastair,' observed Nicola. 'Doesn't he look white, Mum, like a fish and chip paper left out in the rain.'

'Is something the matter, darling?' asked Mum, in alarm.

'Not really –'

He was on the verge of telling them. It might have helped. But their unsympathetic voices came blundering in.

'He's inventing a time theory,' teased Chris, 'and the brainwork's wearing him out.'

'Maybe he's in love, like Mum said,' suggested Nicola.

Alastair blazed into fury at their incomprehension and stupidity.

'Don't get at him,' Mum was protesting. 'But seriously, Alastair, you do look tired.'

'Of course I'm tired!' he exploded. 'Anyone'd be tired if they'd trogged down to the Fleece two hundred years ago, with mud and stones all over the road, and no lights, and watched an exciseman weigh guineas because

52

he was trying to catch the yellow traders, and then seen James Quarmby snitch some to be clipped at Whinnerah Clough, and wanting to stop him because Martha was getting dead scared, and falling downstairs in a stinking old cloak, so that it was too late; and knowing all the time that he could be hanged, because even people as young as us could be in those days, and then Martha wouldn't have anyone left, since her father drove over the precipice. And it's all boiling around in my head; worry about James, and Martha too if they find the coin ...'

He heard his voice running faster and faster, and rising desperately, as their solid blocks of disbelief seemed to build a wall against him, which he could never surmount.

'I think I'll go to bed,' he finished abruptly.

'Good idea,' said Mum.

She murmured something to Dad in anxious tones, about thermometers, and Paracetamol, but he didn't want to hear. As he dragged himself away, he saw Chris, Nicola and Louise staring after him in open-mouthed astonishment.

10

Never again, thought Alastair, when he woke next morning.

He remembered his wild outburst, the startled faces in the sitting-room, Mum shaking the thermometer and pushing pills at him – and he felt hot with embarrassment. If going back into the past meant another fuss like that, he'd better forget it. Full stop.

He went downstairs to meet Mum's concerned look, the careful kindness of his sisters (amazing from Nicola. She must have had a shock!), and Chris's over-rumbustious cheeriness. They didn't mention second sight, or seeing through time, and nor did he. He hoped the subject was closed and nailed down for good. Indeed, he found himself wondering if he would ever again take out the clipped coin, that launching pad into the past. He simply couldn't decide.

He couldn't decide about a lot of things, his promise to Martha included. For he had promised, in an indefinite sort of way, to help her – there was no point in kidding himself that he hadn't – and he didn't want to be a person who broke his word. Only, did a promise count, if it was given in another century? And wasn't whatever happened to Martha fixed already in the concrete of two hundred historical years, so that his going back, or not, couldn't alter things by so much as a microdot?

But the vague promise went on nagging at him.

Every night in bed his mind tracked back obsessively

to his time-travel adventures. During the day, he plunged resolutely into everything modern. He made posters for a school Green Group project, he experimented with the electronic keyboard, and he borrowed Chris's mountain bike for a ride over the hills – though not up to Whinnerah Clough. He ate more burgers and pizzas than he really enjoyed, and watched a lot of television.

And he missed his computer. How mad to have set it up in the Gable Room! But he didn't want to risk going up and fetching it.

Then, one wet evening, he came home from school with an idea for a new program buzzing through his head. Everyone else was busy – Mum and Dad wallpapering the cloakroom, Chris on a training run, Nicola gossiping down the phone to friends she'd gossiped with all day, Louise soaking up 'The Sound of Music' on video for the seventeenth time. Alastair wanted his computer.

There was only one thing to do. He must screw up his courage, and get it. Nobody could *make* him take the coin out of the crack.

Thinking about the Gable Room, he had almost forgotten what happened on the stairs. He soon remembered. The petrifying chill surged over him like cold water, and, through it, he seemed to hear Martha calling him, with panic in her voice.

Abandoning his computer, he rushed to the crack, and scrabbled the coin out somehow with his fingernail. The old bedroom, swinging back into focus, was empty, but candlelight gleamed from the staircase. Martha was huddled on the sixth step, next to the window, her tear-marked face pressed to the narrow pane.

'James! James!' she wept, and then 'Alastair! Where are you?'

'I'm here.'

He sprang down, and she caught at him, and clung

for a moment as if she couldn't let go. Then, abruptly, she pushed him away, and stared at him with accusing eyes.

'Why have you been so long?' she cried. 'I needed you.'

'It was only a few days –'

'Weeks!' she interrupted. 'Terrible, long, endless weeks. Why did you not come to me?'

'I've been away,' he said. Away in time, not space, but she could take it how she liked.

Satisfied perhaps – he wasn't sure – she whirled round, and gazed out again through the window, her roughened fingers gripping the ledge.

'Martha, what's the matter?'

She looked back, and her face was ghost-white.

'Do you mind how you promised to help me? I need you to keep your promise, you see. Oh, I've been calling and calling to you, as loud as I dared, and I feared you'd never come. But now you have, thank God. It's James. There's danger, and he must be warned, but I can't do it myself. I ran down to the Fleece last night – .'

'What happened?' prompted Alastair, for she had stopped.

'I couldn't find him,' she answered desolately. 'And when I came home, Mrs Gledhill took my shoes and hid them, since I'd gone without asking her leave.'

Glancing down, Alastair saw that her feet were bare.

'What's the danger?'

'They've been on about the yellow traders in the kitchen. Folks are saying there's something – not right – at the farm in Whinnerah Clough. If that's what the servants say, Mr Gledhill could happen hear of it, and he's a magistrate. He knows the law, and he owns Owlsnap, so they chose him for a justice. And he doesn't like James and me. He's fair guilty because he's wronged us, because Owlsnap should be ours. He'd be glad to see James in trouble.'

'D'you want me to find James, then?' asked Alastair doubtfully.

Her face brightened with relief.

'If you could . . .'

'What do you want me to say to him?'

'Tell him to do no more errands to Whinnerah Clough. Tell him to keep away. His life's worth more to me – aye, and to him too – than Owlsnap, or all the gold he might get. I can bear even the Gledhills' malice, if I know James is safe. He's all that's left to me, Alastair, and I can't lose him. Help me!'

'I'll go down to the Fleece, and speak to him at once.'

But she snatched his hand before he could move.

'Not there. Happen someone might hear you. If 'twas the landlord, he'd be mad with rage at you, and if 'twas another, he might betray James. Nay, you must keep away from the inn, fair away. James will be bound for Whinnerah Clough tonight. I've watched, and I know which nights the landlord sends him. Will you meet him in the lane, and stop him?'

Alastair's heart sank. Beyond the window, white moonlight tipped the black hills. He pictured the rough, dark track, the gang of villains . . .

Then Martha's fingers tightened in a despairing grip, and he knew he had no choice.

'Right,' he said. 'I'll go. But I'm not borrowing that cloak again.'

In fact, he didn't need it. Although in the twentieth century it had been raining, the eighteenth century boasted clear weather with a full moon.

Alastair stole out of the house, and made his way cautiously round to the lane. Looking back, he saw a few lights glinting from Owlsnap's irregular windows, with a candle spark under its highest gable. Alastair raised

57

a hand, in case Martha could see him, and then wondered uneasily if there were other watchers. Probably it would be safest to move on a little way. He set off up the hill.

As he walked, an idea struck him. Why not go the whole way, and take a peep, under cover of darkness, at Whinnerah Clough Farm? He needn't get too close, and he could turn straight back and meet James. Feeling both alarmed and excited, but above all determined to be brave, he quickened his pace, and strode on.

All around him was moonlight, and silence broken by the occasional slither of stones underfoot, or the tearing wrench of shadowy sheep cropping grass. He remembered hearing that they had to eat twenty-three hours out of twenty-four. How odd that sheep were just the same two hundred years ago, when people were so different. He found himself contrasting, once again, the ragged fragility of Martha with Nicola's smartness and toughness, and dreamy James with self-assured Chris.

The track rounded a curve, and Alastair saw below him, in a hollow, a solitary house. Whinnerah Clough Farm! The moonlight picked out a long, low roof, and shuttered windows. It looked eerie, secretive. Alastair took a fresh grip on his courage, and moved stealthily on.

The rasping bark of a dog tore through the silence, and there was a rattle, as if it had rushed to the end of a chain, and been choked back. Alastair froze. One of the shutters was noiselessly eased open.

'That you, James, lad?' hissed a voice.

There was no answer. Two or three heads crowded at the window, and Alastair felt his heart jerk in his chest. They were like the heads of mutants in a horror film, oddly-shaped, lumpy and horrible.

'It's the moon,' said another voice, more loudly. 'A full moon can drive dogs mad.'

'Bring him inside,' advised a third, 'or he'll happen rip up our packboy.'

A burst of cruel laughter greeted this, followed by a rattle, a snarl and a curse, as the dog was hauled inside. The door slammed shut.

Alastair turned and ran.

As he reached the corner, he saw a twinkle of light coming up the track. Hooves scraped, and a bridle jingled. Was it James or a coiner? Alastair shrank onto the grass beside the lane. Then the twinkle grew to a lantern's beam, revealing, to Alastair's relief, James's pale, pointed face, and the long, uncombed twists of his hair.

He was riding a spindly pony, which ambled along, loose-reined. The lantern was tied in front of the saddle, with a heavy bag bumping against it. James seemed to have no concern, either for his pony, or for what was, presumably, the landlord's gold. His eyes were fixed on the sky. Even when Alastair stepped forward, saying, 'Just a minute, please,' James was slow to refocus his attention, and glance down at whoever had taken hold of his reins.

'What's to do?' he asked, quite unafraid.

If I was him, I'd have the sense to be a bit scared, thought Alastair.

'You're James Quarmby, aren't you?' he asked.

'Aye.'

'I've come from Martha.'

'Martha? Is aught wrong?'

James's voice actually sharpened into real alarm.

'There's plenty wrong,' said Alastair, 'like cold, and loneliness, and cruelty, and even starvation. But that's not why I'm here. She wants me to tell you that you're to stop taking gold to Whinnerah Clough.'

He felt James stiffen.

'Martha knows why I come,' he said.

'She knows it's dangerous,' returned Alastair.

'Danger's no matter,' said James.

And the awful thing was, thought Alastair, that it didn't matter to him. He really didn't understand the danger. That James's life was in peril every time he carried gold to the yellow traders, seemed the last thing on his mind.

'Don't be such a fool!' said Alastair. 'You should think about what you're doing, for Martha's sake if not your own. Suppose there's a raid on Whinnerah Clough Farm, and you're caught there?'

James shrugged.

'I'll chance it.'

'Why?' demanded Alastair.

'They pay me. In the end I'll be able to buy back my own home.'

'But, don't you see, you're being paid with false gold? They're coiners at the farm, you know, yellow traders. They're clipping guineas to make fakes, and passing the clipped ones back to you. That one you gave Martha is much too small. I've proved it. So the people who are paying you are crooks.'

He spelled out each damning detail, hoping to penetrate the cloak of unreality in which James had shrouded himself, but it was no good.

'True guineas, clipped ones? What's the difference? You can still use them,' said James.

'Not legally!' Alastair shouted. 'Why d'you think the exciseman came into the Fleece with his scales? Illegal guineas are too light.'

'Most people haven't got scales,' James observed.

'So you think it's all right, then?' Alastair was furious. 'You don't think it matters what you pile up, as long as it's golden, and roughly circular. Other people think it matters.'

'There's naught in the world that matters,' said James, 'save buying back Owlsnap. Who are you, anyway?'

'A friend,' said Alastair, 'with a serious warning.'

'Oh, fiddlesticks!' cried James suddenly. 'I'll hear no more of your talk.'

He snatched back the reins, dug his heels into the pony, and cantered away towards the farm.

Alastair stared after him, defeated by the enormous gulf between his own time and James's. Stuck in his village, with no contact with the world outside, and possibly no education, to teach him what real life was about, James was like a blind man on a tightrope, fated for disaster. Money clearly had little meaning to him, if he couldn't see the difference between false and genuine coins, and if he believed he could scramble enough together to buy back Owlsnap from the entrenched Gledhills. And such foolishness could lead him to his death.

But then he had no idea about self-protection. If somebody stopped me in the dark, like I stopped him, Alastair reflected, I'd expect a mugging. No such thought had crossed James's mind. He wandered about, absurdly trustful, with no more doubts about shifty landlords and yellow traders than he had about his own ridiculous plans. If he wasn't on a tightrope, he was walking in his sleep.

At least I'm usually on the ball, Alastair decided. And then he wondered what the coiners were really like.

All this time he was watching James ride up to the farm. Someone came out and spoke to him. Coins clinked. James turned the pony, and rode off along the far side of the hollow. He didn't want to meet Alastair again.

Alastair let him go. He had noticed that the shutter, which had been opened earlier, had not been properly closed. The temptation to sneak up and peep in was overwhelming.

Cautiously, Alastair approached the house. Stone built, stone roofed, it huddled into the moorland hills, perfect, thought Alastair wryly, for a crime serial on television. Edging past some spiky rosebushes, he crept to the unfastened shutter, and peered into the room beyond.

The contrast with the darkened hillside was staggering!

Dozens of candles blazed from silver candlesticks, and a huge fire roared up the chimney. Lit by the brilliance, a number of people were grouped round the room. Handfuls of guineas had been tumbled onto a white sheet spread across a table, and a grinning man was holding the strong-bladed shears with which he was about to clip them. Another lounged beside him, tipping back a bottle, and laughing, with such a jeering look on his face, that Alastair immediately hated him. Two others were playing cards among a debris of plates and tankards.

They were all dressed to a pitch of grandeur equalled only in a pantomine, thought Alastair, astonished. Indeed, their elaborate clothes made them seem more like actors than real people. The men wore brightly coloured coats trimmed with gold lace, and their heads, which had looked so sinister at the window, were crowned with wigs, rolled into tight bunches of curls round the ears. There were a couple of women too, in low-cut dresses, whose jewellery flashed as they fanned themselves. One of the card players pinched some powder from a little box, and held it to his nostrils, sneezing explosively. Snuff, gasped Alastair to himself.

He had never expected the yellow traders to be like this. He had imagined them lean and haggard, like the men in the Fleece. But the coiners had grown fat on their riches. Embroidered waistcoats wrinkled round their bulging stomachs. Silk stockings sagged from swollen calves. Money had been lavished on the furnishings too. There was a thick carpet on the floor, and along the panelled walls hung heavy, gilt-framed portraits of stately people. One of them, a judge, had had his nose enlarged with a disrespectful slap of paint, and his mouth turned up in a silly red grin.

'How much has the lad brought?' inquired the snuff-taker, who seemed to be the eldest.

'Thirty-two,' answered the man with the shears, counting.

'Ah! Forty pennorth of gold clipped off each of thirty-two. That's four new guineas for us, lads. Not bad,' said the snuff-taker, rubbing his hands.

A woman in emerald satin minced over, and tapped the old man on the wig with her fan.

'I want some diamond buckles, mind.'

'You never cease wanting,' he growled.

'You are my example, sir.'

She picked up a bottle, drank, and belched.

'Hey!' The man with the jeering laugh, who had been running the coins through his fingers, flung one on the floor in disgust. 'This here's a dud! It's been clipped before.'

'I'll clip it again,' the shearsman offered.

'Nay, you won't. It'd not pass for a half guinea, never name more. Wait till I catch that lad! Bringing us clipped gold –'

'He weren't to blame,' interrupted the shearsman mildly. 'But you've always got your knife in him, Walter.'

'Well, and ain't it natural? Have you forgot his father already? I've not forgot him, and the deal of money he was owing me when he chucked hisself off Morthwaite

63

Heights. Cut and run, that were Thomas Quarmby. Of all the crooked, swindling gamesters I'd ever the ill luck to meet, he was the crookedest. He'd hold on to your guineas longer nor life. He proved it, didn't he? I'll wager that lad of his knew right well what he were doing. He'd some fine trick in mind to diddle us, just like his dad. Well, he won't get away with it, not this time. He'll pay for it, I'll make damn sure of that. He'll –.'

Seizing a bottle, the man hurled it at the crack between the shutters.

Alastair ducked, just in time. The bottle whizzed past, lodging in the thorny embrace of a rosebush, and Alastair flew for his life.

11

How he covered the ground between Whinnerah Clough and Owlsnap, and got back into the house and the Gable Room, Alastair couldn't afterwards remember. He had a brief memory of Martha, jerking upright in bed as he burst in, and then he forced the coin into the crack, and made for the stairs.

In his haste, he misjudged their steepness. He tripped, stumbled, and plunged headlong down, ending in a knotted heap outside Nicola's door.

For a moment he couldn't move. He lay stunned and breathless, reflecting that time travel and stairs didn't seem to mix. Then gradually he began to sort himself out, gingerly extracting a twisted arm from behind his back, and a bruised ankle from under the opposite knee. His ankle was agony!

He sat on the floor, telling himself that rubbing might help, and almost feeling the injury swelling beneath his fingers. After a bit, he dragged himself into Nicola's room, and crashed out on her bed.

It would have to be Nicola's bed, of course! He opened his eyes, and saw her standing over him.

'You here again! What's the idea?'

'I was going up to the Gable Room – my computer – I fell . . .'

His voice came out in a muffled bleat, like a sheep that ate for twenty-three hours, a sheep near Whinnerah Clough. He shut his eyes, and heard Nicola's footsteps pelting to the door, and her frightened shriek.

'Mum! Quick! Something awful's happened to Alastair.'

In the end, it wasn't that awful. Dad loaded him into the car, and drove him to hospital, where his ankle was pronounced badly sprained, but not broken. It was mummified in a tight web of strapping, and he was sent home with instructions to keep it up, and not put any weight on it for a few days.

'At least he's not sporty,' said Chris.

They were all standing round his bed, and discussing him as if he was a corpse.

'He won't be able to go to school,' Nicola pointed out.

'Lucky Alastair!' sighed Louise.

'I'd better stay at home too. He'll need looking after,' said Mum.

'Aren't your 'mocks' just coming up?' asked Dad.

'Oh, yes.'

'They'll need you at school, then. Alastair'll be OK on his own. You can leave him lunch, and a drink. Kids don't need mollycoddling,' said Dad.

Mollycoddling might actually have been rather nice, Alastair reflected next morning, when they'd all gone off, and he was left on the sofa downstairs, with a sandwich box, a packet of crisps, an apple, two cans of Coke and a Mars Bar, to see him through the long day – as well as an aching ankle. But there it was. He could have television or a video, read or draw, or just lie and think.

He lay and thought.

From the churning medley of pictures, which the evening's adventure had left in his head, he pulled out one or two for closer examination. First there were the coiners of Whinnerah Clough, in their wigs and satins. He still found their showy spendour incredible. But why should he? Didn't criminals the world over revel in what they could buy with their ill-gotten riches?

He remembered Dad talking about the part of Spain which people had nicknamed the Costa del Crime. And there, on hot headlands, between blue seas and bluer skies, big-time crooks and gangsters holed up in fabulous mansions, equipped themselves with swimming pools, jacuzzis, and electronic gadgets barely off the drawing board, stuffed their kitchens with juicy steaks, lobsters and champagne, topped their high white walls with rolls of barbed wire, and settled down to a life of idle luxury.

The yellow traders had done exactly the same, given that they were stuck in an eighteenth century Pennine village.

But they couldn't expect to keep such flaunted wealth a secret for ever, especially in a small community. Sooner or later, someone would notice. They were stupid not to have realized this, stupid and unrealistic. As James was.

In other circumstances, Alastair decided, he might well have liked James. That pointed face with its faraway eyes looked clever; inventive, even. But there was a fatal weakness in James, a bug, wrecking his system. He just didn't see the impossibility of buying Owlsnap back.

Alastair thought of James's reckless father, Thomas Quarmby the gambler. Like James, he was hopelessly unrealistic, staking his house on a cockfight. James must have inherited a blind spot from Thomas, like Chris had inherited sportiness from Dad, and he, Alastair, had inherited second sight from his great-grandmother, now smiling demurely at him from her portrait on the shelf.

'You got me into this,' Alastair told her accusingly.

He began to sketch family trees on a piece of paper; Thomas down to James and Martha; great-grandmother down to Mum and himself. But tiredness from his adventures overcame him, and quite soon he dropped his pencil and let himself flake out.

He stayed on the sofa all weekend, while family life eddied round him. Chris and Dad were in and out to football, or mulling over the League result on Ceefax. Nicola had been asked to a party – 'by the fabbest boy in our year!' she gloated – which meant much public agonizing over clothes, and shoes, and hair, with despair about spilled nail varnish and lost earrings. Louise, who had somehow acquired a forked twig, wanted to go dowsing for the Bottomless Well, and was whiny about the overgrown tangle of the garden.

'Well, I can't do anything about it now,' countered Mum, quite sharply for her. 'You know I've asked these two girls from my school to drop round. They still need a lot of help if they're to have any chance in the exams next week. We've people coming in for drinks tonight, and we haven't *touched* the cloakroom ceiling yet.'

The doorbell pinged, the phone shrilled, cars bumped down the lane, and ground back up it. Alastair lay thinking how the bright bustle of Quarmby Hall had superimposed itself over the troubles and sorrows of Owlsnap, turning them thinner than cobwebs. It was like looking at one of those books where a modern colour shot was placed beside an old black and white photo of the same place; dominating, and so destroying, it.

And he preferred the bustle really, only he felt a bit left out. He had never been so important to anyone as, long ago or last week, he had been to Martha.

He found he was thinking a lot about Martha, and missing her.

It was Chris, of all people, who noticed how alone he was. Coming in from a run, Chris peered round the sitting-room door, said, 'Hi!', disappeared, and came back.

'Are you fed up, stuck here?' he asked.

'A bit,' Alastair admitted.

'You haven't got your computer. You look like Popeye without his spinach. D'you want it?'

'M'm! But it's in the Gable Room.'

'No problem.'

Chris had vanished to fetch it before Alastair could stop him.

Which he might have done, for the possibility of Chris's encountering Martha, blundering, somehow, into her night-moth fragility, seeing her tears and humiliations, suddenly hit him, and scared him rigid. Nobody must know about Martha, except him. Nobody else would understand.

Immediately he began to reassure himself. Chris had been up there before without noticing anything, and it would be easy to miss the clipped gold under the skirting board. But when he heard Chris's feet clattering down the front stairs like a runaway train, he stiffened in terror.

The sitting-room door shot open.

'God!' exclaimed Chris, shuddering to a halt on the hearthrug.

'What's wrong?'

But already the thought had flashed through Alastair's head that, with the false coin's eccentric time scheme, Chris might have paid a long visit to the past, and seen James arrested and executed, in the moments since he set off for the computer.

'There's something definitely odd about those stairs,' said Chris.

Only 'something odd'? Relief!

'What d'you mean?' Alastair asked cautiously.

'Oh, I dunno. I can't explain. For a second it was like going into a freezer. And not just that. There were – sort of – voices.'

He stopped.

'Go on,' Alastair dared to suggest.

'No. No, forget it. It was nothing. I think I got a bit cold on my run. It's nippy out, you know.' He shivered elaborately. 'There's nothing that a hot shower won't cure, but I'd better have one straight away.'

'Don't bother with the computer then,' said Alastair.

'Sure?' Thankfulness beamed in Chris's face.

'Yeah. I've got this magazine to read.'

'OK. Right. I'll scarper.' Yet still Chris hung about the door, looking pinkly embarrassed. 'Don't tell anyone what I said – about the stairs – will you? They'd think I'd flipped my lid. Especially Nicola. You know what she's like.'

Chris laughed half-heartedly.

'I won't say a thing,' Alastair promised.

'Thanks. I'll get your computer another time. Dad can give me a hand. You need two to fetch it down.' He opened the door at last, and then turned back. 'Funny thing. I must be wrong but I could have sworn I heard a voice on the stairs calling your name.'

12

Martha was calling him. Alastair couldn't get the thought out of his mind. It nagged worse than his aching ankle for the rest of the day, and all through the night as he dozed fitfully. He'd slumped too long on the sofa, he told himself, but that was just an excuse. Martha's despair was the real reason why he couldn't sleep.

'You'll need another day off school,' said Mum, seeing his white face. 'Oh dear, I hate leaving you, but I'm down to invigilate.'

'It's OK,' said Alastair.

Some time around five a.m., he had made up his mind. As soon as the family left home, he would drag himself up to the Gable Room somehow, if he had to crawl every centimetre of the way. There might not be much he could do when he got there, but Martha needed him, and he had to go.

When they'd all gone, and he'd got up and dressed, his ankle didn't feel too bad. By hopping and hobbling, he soon reached Nicola's room. He paused, summoned his courage, and opened the far door. The chilling waves of the haunted staircase shocked him anew with their force. But of course they were strong. They'd even penetrated Chris's natural resistance.

'I'm coming, Martha!' he shouted, heaving himself up on hands and knees.

The clipped gold from the crack revealed the old, tragic scene. Martha was crying on the bed. She must, thought Alastair, have shed more tears on the three occasions he'd talked to her, than Nicola had in the last three years. No wonder her face looked so hollowed and wan, as if its substance had drained away while she wept.

'Martha.' He gently touched the thin bones under the quilt. 'It's all right. I'm here. I'll help you.'

She sprang up in bed.

'Alastair!'

And, for the first time, he saw her smile. White and woebegone as she was, her face lit up with a joy that was all for him.

'I knew as you'd come!' she cried.

'Have you been calling long?' he asked.

'Aye. But this time I never lost heart. Not like before. I was mad at you last time, because I hadn't learned I could trust you. I knew I could do that when you went out after James for me – even though he didn't listen to you. Only a friend would have done that. I'll not be mad at you no more, now.'

They were friends! His heart bounded with happiness. But there were more serious matters for his attention.

'Why were you calling?' he said. 'Has James – ?'

'Been caught?' As she completed the sentence for him, the old despair drowned her smile. 'Not yet, but he will be. He's clean daft. He goes to Whinnerah Clough more and more. And tonight –'

'What?' cried Alastair.

'Cook made me take the men's supper out to the stable. A whole gang were gathering; men from the village wi' sticks and pitchforks, and Mr Gledhill's men. One of them knew me, and I knew him. He used to tend Father's cocks in times gone. He gave me a look, and said . . .' She paused. 'He said, "There's another Quarmby marked for his come-uppance. Like father, like son," he said. I flew back to the kitchen, and asked Jacky, the turnspit, where they were bound. He nobbut laughed, and answered, "Whinnerah Clough. Mr Gledhill's bent on knowing what's going on there. The men'll wait till nigh on midnight," Jacky said to me; "then they'll spring".'

'And you think James will be there?'

'Aye – I'm afeared,' she murmured. 'I don't rightly know –'

'We must go and see.' Alastair glanced out of the window at the black sky. 'It's late. We should go now. Or shall I go alone?'

He spoke with a calm that amazed himself. He was scared, but above the alarm was an even stronger feeling, a determination to help Martha.

'Nay, I'll come with you,' she said. 'I stole a pair of Jacky's boots. I were fain to go – even without you. But I'm right glad you came.'

With a swift movement, she leaped off the bed, and threw her frail arms round him. Under the tears, her face looked almost beautiful.

'I think I've known I could trust you,' she said, 'ever since you found my guinea.'

'What's that got to do with it?'

'I made a spell when I hid it,' she explained, 'to protect James. It were a spell I learned off our old nurse, when I was a bairn. So I knew the guinea could only be found by them as'd help us.'

Alastair mentally raised disbelieving eyebrows. Spells were a bit over the top, and totally unscientific. But really, that didn't matter. Something uncanny had brought him to the Gable Room, and to Martha – and how lucky that it had!

'I'll put on the boots. We'd best be going.' Martha fished them out from under the bed, and paused, staring at Alastair's trainers. 'You've some fair queer shoes! Are they from London?'

'Yes.'

Queer shoes for a queer errand. Alastair had no clear idea of what they were going to do. But there was one good thing. His ankle now felt perfectly all right.

'Let's hurry,' said Martha.

She took his hand, and they slipped quietly downstairs, and out into the yard. A lantern glimmered near the back door, as if someone had put it down before going inside.

'We're in luck!' whispered Martha, and, picking it up, she sped off between the old buildings, her will-o'-the-wisp light marking the way.

They hurried along the track, through invisible, munching sheep.

'Who exactly lives at Whinnerah Clough Farm?' asked Alastair.

'It belongs to old Mr Boothroyd. He's grazed his sheep nigh to ours since my father was a lad, and Father'd often say he'd nick ours if he could. Father'd never trust him. There's a whole clan of them, living at the farm; sons and daughters, and that. Mr Walter Boothroyd, the old man's eldest son, kept cocks, like Father.'

'And like Mr Gledhill. Does everyone round here go in for cock-fighting?'

'There's naught else to do in winter, save drinking,' said Martha simply.

'But it's . . .' Alastair stopped. There was no point in telling her that cock-fighting was cruel, that one day, in the future, it would be banned. So he was silent, pondering over the stark dreadfulness of eighteenth century life, when the long winter nights offered, for amusement, a choice between drunkenness and animal torture.

And he remembered the coiner called Walter, Walter Boothroyd, the man who had threatened vengeance on James.

74

A sudden pounding of hooves and jingling of harness made them both jump. A cart was rattling towards them at a fast pace, from the direction of Whinnerah Clough. Alastair grabbed Martha, to pull her off the track, but in the swaying light of the driving lanterns, she had recognized her brother.

'James!' she shrieked.

The cart lurched to a halt. James's face beamed down at them, and his voice was jubilant.

'Martha? Is that you? I've got it, Martha! I've got the gold to buy back Owlsnap!'

'What?' Martha exclaimed.

'Gold! A whole boxful! Look.'

Carelessly dropping the reins, he reached back into the cart. There on the boards was a sturdy wooden box, with brass clasps and corners.

'Is it full of gold?' asked Martha, awestruck.

'Aye. Guineas and half guineas – '

'Hang on.' Alastair stepped forward into the light. 'Where's it come from?'

'Who's that? Oh,' said James. 'You. What d'you want, then?'

'To see inside that box,' Alastair answered grimly.

'Never!'

James swung round again to pick up the reins, but Alastair had already seized them.

'Sorry,' he said, 'but I can't let you go charging off with a load of clipped gold. It'd be like tying the rope round your neck.'

'Who the devil is your fine lad with the mincing voice, Martha?' James demanded.

Thanks for the compliment, thought Alastair, and he spoke up before Martha could reply.

'I'm staying at Owlsnap, and Martha's told me all about you. The gold comes from Whinnerah Clough, doesn't it?'

'Aye,' agreed James defiantly, 'given me as a present by a right generous friend. You mind Mr Walter Booth-royd, Martha, who came to Owlsnap many a time when Father was living? He called me into the farmhouse tonight, and said he were fair fretted to hear of our troubles. And then he showed me the box of gold on the cart, and told me to take it to Mr Gledhill, and say it were the price for Owlsnap.'

'You *fool!*' cried Alastair. 'You supersonic nutcase! He's sending you to your death.'

'Oh, no!' gasped Martha.

Alastair rounded on her.

'But he is. You said yourself that old Mr Boothroyd was untrustworthy. Don't you see? It's just a trick. The yellow traders have heard that they may be raided, so they've offloaded the clipped gold on to James.'

'What do you know about it?' snapped James. 'I trust the Boothroyds. Nay, Mr Walter Boothroyd said as he'd read in his Bible that Christian charity should be prac-tised secret-like, and he'd rather not take credit for help-ing us, Martha. So if Mr Gledhill happen asks where the gold comes from, I'm not to name him, but say as how a friend brought it for us, from over Lancashire way. I thought it were right good of him to be so modest.'

Alastair stared incredulously. And he'd imagined James might be clever! A nine-year-old like Louise wouldn't have been taken in by that kind of trick.

'It wasn't good. It was downright cunning and deceit-ful,' he began.

And at that moment, they heard footsteps and horses coming up the track from Owlsnap.

'Quick! Let's get out of the way!' hissed Alastair, and he tugged at the reins, pulling the cart away onto tussocks of heather.

'What – ?' began James.

'Ssh!' Halting the cart, Alastair threw his arm round the horse's muzzle, to prevent it from neighing.

'Cover the lamps,' he directed, but Martha had already done so, burying them under her shawl.

If James speaks, or the harness jingles, we'll be caught red-handed, he thought despairingly. Then he realized that the posse from Owlsnap were making such a din themselves, with trampling hooves and boots, that their own small noises were drowned. They stood frozen as the men hurried past, and on towards Whinnerah Clough.

'There!' said Alastair, when the last sounds had died away. 'They're off to ransack the farm. They're after the clipped gold, James.'

'Oh, fiddlesticks!' snorted James. 'And what if they are? Who's to tell if their gold's clipped or not?'

'I can tell,' returned Alastair. 'The clipped guinea you gave Martha is here in my pocket. If the guineas in that box are the same size, they could send you to the gallows.'

'Will you look, Alastair?' begged Martha, in such a terrified voice, that he wished he hadn't said 'gallows'. But it was done now.

'Right,' he said soberly. 'And you must look too.'

Alastair hoisted himself on to the cart, and pulled Martha up beside him. Then he unclasped the lid of the box, and lifted it. As Martha snatched her shawl off the lamps, a heaped pile of gold twinkled, bright and deadly, under their eyes.

'Oh!' breathed Martha faintly.

Even Alastair was shaken. It was the kind of hoard over which a story-book dragon might have sprawled and puffed – not the sort of thing he had ever expected to see in real life. No wonder ignorant James believed it would buy back Owlsnap. But it was vital to stay cool about it.

'I'll measure one,' he said.

He took out the Gable Room guinea, and was holding it over the box, when James suddenly cracked his whip, and the cart plunged forward, with a lurch that jolted the coin out of his fingers. It spun down on top of the others, and there was no time to pick it out, for James had urged the horse into a gallop, and the cart was bouncing and thumping over the ruts, so that Alastair and Martha had to cling to the sides, to save themselves from hurtling out.

'James!' screamed Martha. 'Stop!'

'Not till I've got the gold to Owlsnap.'

And James lashed the horse relentlessly on.

'We mustn't let him take the gold to Mr Gledhill,' cried Martha.

'No. We won't.'

Letting go with one hand, Alastair slammed and fastened the lid.

The cart rocketed round the corner of Owlsnap, swinging perilously between barns and stables. Alastair calculated his moment, kicked the box off the end of the cart, and jumped out after it.

The crash of the gold alerted James. He dropped the reins and sprang down before Alastair had time to recover himself.

'Give me my gold!' he screamed.

'No chance.'

The cart, with Martha still aboard, clattered away, its disappearing lamps leaving the yard in thick darkness.

Alastair had never felt so frightened and alone. The stench of muck and horses was stifling, and the unfamiliar buildings hemmed him in. He bent to grab the box, and escape with it somewhere – anywhere – just as James's fingers clutched at his collar. He lashed out fiercely, hurling James against a stone wall. Alastair heard the thud of his fall, but there was no time for sympathy. He must hide the box before James was on his feet again.

'Alastair!'

Martha's shriek rang across the yard. She too must have leaped from the cart, and was running to help him.

'Where are you?' he shouted.

And then, as moonlight blazed suddenly down from a gap in the clouds, he caught sight of her, beckoning frantically to him from beside a low wall.

'I'm here. Quick!' she called.

He seized the box's brassbound end, and dragged it swiftly towards her, over the slippery, muddy cobbles. The fear that James might at any moment pounce on him out of the shadows seemed to lend him incredible strength.

'It's the well!' Martha cried. 'Throw the box down!'

Heaving it up onto the edge of the well, he pushed as hard as he could – and realized immediately what he had done. The coin from the Gable Room was amongst the hoard, splashing down into the bottomless depth of water; his time-travel passport, his way home. Without it, he could be stuck in Owlsnap for ever, condemned to cold, and fear, and shadows, barred from his own family.

He flung himself forward, trying vainly to snatch back the falling box.

'Alastair!' Martha screamed. 'Take care!'

And she stretched her thin, ghostly hands out to him.

But the box plunged downwards, and he seemed to plunge after it. Moonlight, darkness, and the fathomless pit of the well whirled round him. He caught one last glimpse of Martha's face, wild and despairing.

He closed his eyes.

13

When he opened them again he was sitting on a sharp-edged stone, in a jungle of brambles and small thrusting saplings. Overhead shone the pale, February sun, and beyond the tangled scrub rose the old grey walls of Quarmby Hall.

Quarmby Hall, not Owlsnap, because the back door, which he could see, was daffodil yellow.

'The place needs a bit of brightening up,' Dad had said, creaming on the paint soon after they'd arrived.

So, somehow, he was back.

The stone was cold and uncomfortable. He stood up without thinking, and a knifeblade of pain sliced through his ankle.

'Ow!' he yelled, and hearing his voice, Mitt the Kitt pushed her tabby face between tufts of shrivelled grass. He picked her up and hugged her.

With the cat in his arms, he hobbled back to the house, and flopped on to the sofa. His lunchbox and his computer magazines were stacked on the coffee table. Everything around him was bright and warm, cosy and attractive. Yet when he remembered cold, candlelit, fear-filled Owlsnap, he could have wept with sorrow because he had lost it.

For he had lost it. He didn't see how he could ever return. And that meant he'd lost Martha.

Odd how that little, frail, phantom girl, with her funny, old-fashioned way of speaking, had wound herself round his heart; so that – he might as well admit it – she meant more to him than anyone had ever done before; because she had needed him, and called to him, and thrown arms light as cobwebs around him.

Oh, Martha!

The doorbell pealed. Who could that be? He limped out and opened it, and saw the thin, Sherlock Holmes face of Tony Elland. He was muffled in a scarf, and carrying a cardboard folder.

'Hi,' he said. 'I heard you were laid up, so I thought I'd drop by and say hello.'

'How did you hear?' asked Alastair, surprised.

'Things get round in a village.'

He came into the hall, unwinding his scarf.

'I remembered you were interested in the coiners, so I thought you might like to read my article. It'd pass a bit of time for you. Here.'

He held out the folder.

Alastair froze. He most certainly did not want to read it. Lurking inside that harmless-looking envelope might be details of James's execution.

'I'm not really into history,' he said stiffly.

'History sounds dull,' agreed Tony, 'but, at bottom, it's just stories about people, not so very different from what you read in the newspapers or get on TV today. I mean,' and he walked into the sitting-room, so that Alastair had to follow, 'what astonished me, was discovering how the yellow traders had splurged out with their faked coins, to provide for what was, in those days, an extremely cushy lifestyle. At least, I was astonished at first. But then I thought they were only like lots of other people. They wanted to get rich quick, and live the good life.'

Alastair felt an urge to snap back, 'I know!' More strongly, he wanted to say, 'Shut up, and go away'. Instead, he was silent.

81

'The coiners' family name was Boothroyd,' Tony went on. 'They called themselves yeomen farmers, but they were really petty thieves and sheep rustlers. How exactly they got into coining, I haven't discovered. They must have wished they hadn't when they paid for it with their necks. The father, and his eldest son, Walter, were hanged in York, and two other sons and their wives were transported to Australia.'

He pulled out his papers, and flicked casually through them.

'Was that all?' Alastair croaked.

'All?'

'No one else was punished?'

'No. The landlord of the Fleece was suspected, but there wasn't enough proof to bring him to trial, and nobody else was involved.'

Alastair let out a long, long sigh.

'It seems to have been quite difficult getting evidence at all,' said Tony. 'The local magistrate sent his men to raid the farm on –' he consulted his article, 'February 16th 1761, but they didn't find anything incriminating, apart from a general appearance of extraordinary wealth, which the coiners explained as being the gift of an anonymous friend from Lancashire.' (They would, thought Alastair!) 'However, there was another raid a year later, and that time the coiners were caught with their shears and their pile of gold.'

So February 16th 1761, reflected Alastair, was the day he'd seized the box of gold, and chucked it down the well, nearly drowning himself in the process. And that was the last time he'd seen Martha. Somehow it felt rather comforting to know the actual date.

'D'you want some coffee?' he asked. Operating the percolator was a fun thing to do, and a distraction from the turmoil of emotions inside him.

'If you can manage it,' said Tony, eyeing his bandaged ankle.

'I'm fine,' said Alastair.

And he walked quite briskly into the kitchen, with Tony in tow.

'Marvellous old room!' observed Tony, staring round.

Alastair nearly remarked that it hadn't been so marvellous in 1761, but he stifled the words, smiling to himself.

'I've been doing some research on Quarmby Hall too,' Tony continued, 'or Owl Snape, as it was called till long after the Quarmbys left.'

Staring at the percolator, Alastair dared to ask, 'Do you know what happened to Thomas Quarmby's children?'

'Ah, yes. They were called James and Martha, and late in 1761 – the same year, coincidentally, as the unsuccessful raid on Whinnerah Clough, though of course there's no connection – they emigrated to America.'

'Is that right?' exclaimed Alastair, startled.

'Yes. A vicar who'd recently come to the parish encouraged emigration for people in distress. It was a way of beginning a new life, which I suppose was what the young Quarmbys needed, orphaned and homeless as they were.'

'If we could get away!' Martha had cried. *'Over the hills and far away, with Owlsnap left behind for ever.'* And they had!

Carefully expressionless, but inwardly bubbling, Alastair got milk from the fridge, and poured two cups of coffee.

'But there's something I want to follow up,' said Tony, hooking out a stool from under the table. 'It's the question of the haunted staircase.'

Alastair's rising cheerfulness crash-landed.

'What d'you mean?'

'I've picked out some odd references as I've been researching; mentions in old letters and things. Here's one.' And he read aloud from a notebook. '"Among haunted houses in Yorkshire, rumour tells of a staircase at Quarmby Hall, mounting to a chamber under the gable, where the piteous cries of a young girl may be heard, and the chill of her ghostly presence felt." That was written in 1852. And a few years later somebody else described how he "encountered on an attic staircase at Quarmby Hall a phantom child, who moaned aloud in woe and desolation."' Tony closed his notebook. 'My suspicion is that people had been reading *Wuthering Heights* – the famous story by Emily Bronte, you know – and attached a ghost, like the one in that book, to another old Yorkshire house. But there may be more to it than that.'

Alastair swallowed. 'You reckon?' he muttered.

'I'm not sure, but I'd love to investigate those stairs. I've thought before that there are strange vibes in this house. In fact, I should confess, that's really why I came, though of course I wanted to cheer you up too. Your parents won't mind if I just have a peep, will they?'

What could he say? His parents wouldn't mind, but Alastair himself was horrified. Investigate poor Martha? Track her down? Play games with her sad shade? At least the lost coin would prevent Sherlock Tony from seeing her – or he hoped it would! – but if Chris had sensed her presence, Tony would be sure to do so. And he didn't want anybody to know about her, disturb her, upset her. He desperately didn't want it.

For a moment, wild ideas about creating a diversion flew through his head. He could knock over the coffee, stage a faint. But no. Better, maybe, to go upstairs and by pretending he felt nothing, convince Tony that any vibes were purely imaginary. *If* he could pretend, with

Martha's petrifying force targeting him.

'This way,' he gulped.

The first link of the haunted stairs twisted above them. There was the narrow window from which she had seen her father galloping to his death, and watched in terror for James. There was the dreaded sixth step.

'Ankle OK?' chirruped Tony, breezing upwards. He passed the window, and climbed on up.

Alastair paused, senses alert. Sunlight fell gently through the window on to bare wooden boards. Around him, the old house creaked and hummed faintly. There was no chill, no ghost, just peace and warmth. Martha had gone.

'This is a let-down!' Tony called from above. 'Someone must have exorcized the poor girl.' He clattered back into view. 'I think I'll have to write an article on the lost phantom of Owl Snape.'

'Owlsnap,' corrected Alastair, without thinking.

'Funny you should say that,' observed Tony. 'I believe Owlsnap was actually the old pronunciation. Shall we go down? Another coffee might quench my disappointment. I've had some very successful ghost-hunts in the past.'

14

It was May, and the late afternoon sunshine trailed golden light over the hillside. Coming up the lane from school, Alastair marvelled at how the landscape had changed. Where, all through winter, the ground had been colourless and dead, brilliant new grass was rampaging, and even the dark, crooked bulk of Quarmby Hall was humanized when bright spring flowers fringed its stone walls.

Not that he still thought of Quarmby Hall as alarming. After living there for five months, he was used to it; was, in fact, rather proud of his picturesque home.

He'd been out a lot lately, though, because he'd joined the school Caving Club, and they were preparing for a big pot-holing expedition. Alastair was looking forward to it. He loved the idea of the underground world, with its linking passages and chambers, its stalactites and stalagmites, and deep subterranean streams. Its geography and geology were solid and understandable. You could explore it systematically, and map it properly. Not like going back in time. But he checked himself. He didn't think about Martha if he could help it.

Cloud shadows drifted across the field beneath the house, and there were other, unfamiliar shadows too. The sun's May angle exposed details which the winter light had failed to pick out. That dark hollow, scooped from the side of the hill, for instance. Alastair paused and stared, trying to make out what it was. An arena? No, it was too small. A pit? Of course! It was the cockpit; that fatal spot where Thomas Quarmby had wagered Owlsnap, and lost it for ever.

The question which had been bugging him since February, in spite of his efforts to smother it, came streaking back. Had they been true, those visits into the long forgotten past? Or had they, as the cool scientific side of his personality kept suggesting, been only imaginary?

Often he told himself he must have been fantasizing. He'd been lonely and uneasy, in an old house with a strange atmosphere, and so he'd let his imagination rip. That was all. Then he saw something like the cockpit, and logical explanations were shattered. Because then he knew that he really had seen Martha; had seen her, loved her, and lost her.

He turned away from the cockpit, and walked on up the hill.

He'd just reached the gate when a piercing shriek rang out from somewhere nearby. Alastair jumped – then knew that it couldn't be Martha. As a second shriek followed, he recognized Louise's voice, coming from behind Quarmby Hall. He tore round the house to see what was happening.

Dad still hadn't found time to start on the back garden, and, with spring, the tangle of bushes and briars flourished like an equatorial jungle.

'I must do something,' Dad said, night after night, but the garden at the front claimed his attention first, or he went off with Chris to cricket practice, or drove Nicola to a disco, while Mum groaned over a pile of marking. So the fact that Alastair couldn't see Louise at once wasn't surprising.

He called out, and with a flurry of branches, she burst from the undergrowth.

'Oh, Alastair, come quick. It's Mitt the Kitt. She's fallen down a hole. I saw her disappear.'

87

And the branches swung together as Louise vanished.

Alastair pushed his way after her, shielding his face from brambles, and arrived in a little stony space, beneath the twisting arms of a hawthorn tree. Close to its trunk, Louise was crouching on hands and knees.

'Look!' she said, pointing.

Alastair bent down. The tree rose out of a rubble of stones, and a mat of ferns and grasses, but Louise held back the fronds, and he saw, under the tree roots, a hole, dropping into blackness.

'It's the Bottomless Well,' said Louise.

Alastair felt his blood run cold.

'Are you sure?'

'Yes. My hazel twig kept twitching round here, that time I was dowsing. But, you see, it's completely hidden by all these plants.'

'You could be right,' said Alastair slowly. 'These stones might be parts of the well wall, smashed up by the tree roots.'

He saw that well wall quite clearly, with Martha beside it. He remembered her face, and how she'd stretched out her hands to save him.

'Mitt the Kitt's down there,' wailed Louise.

'Let's have a look.'

Alastair parted the ferns, and stared down. At first he could only see darkness. Then, as his eyes adjusted, he saw twin specks of light, which resolved themselves into two sharp yellow cat's eyes. Mitt the Kitt was crouching on a jutting stone, a little below the mouth of the well. Her face showed the same happy, complacent expression it always wore when she'd perched herself somewhere unusual, like in the bath, or under a duvet, or aloft on a high cupboard top.

'She's OK,' he said.

'In that hole? She can't be! Poor Mitt!'

'She is,' said Alastair.

'No, she's stuck. Oh, Mitty! Mitty!'

A swift scrabbling of paws, a flattening of fern fronds, and Mitt the Kitt landed beside them. She pushed her face through the grass towards Louise.

'I bet she's often been down there before,' said Alastair.

'Well, she mustn't go again. She might have fallen ever so far.'

'Cats don't.'

'You're being horrid to her. I shall find her some tea.'

With Mitt the Kitt in her arms, Louise wriggled away, Alastair stayed where he was. He remembered that sharp-edged stone beside him, and how Mitt the Kitt had appeared just at the end of his last time-travel adventure, and he knew with absolute certainty that Louise was right. The hole under the tree roots was the Bottomless Well.

A daring plan began to form itself in his head; a plan for going back.

Martha would be glad to see him. She'd wanted them to be friends, and that counted for more than all the terrors of Owlsnap, from which part of him shrank.

'*Take care!*' she had called, as if he really mattered to her.

He sat under the hawthorn tree for a while, considering. Then he opened his school bag, and took out a torch. A powerful light was an essential part of his Caving Club gear, and Dad had got him a fabulous one. Stooping between the ferns, he shone the bright beam down the well.

It glistened on damp, ancient walls, lining the shaft. Lumps of stone, like the one on which Mitt the Kitt had squatted, projected here and there, and strange, slimy plants and mosses sprouted. Unsavoury smells of moisture and decay drifted upwards, but, ignoring them,

Alastair held his torch steady, letting his eyes focus properly through the gloom.

And suddenly he saw it.

Far, far below, the wooden box lay sideways, across a ledge of rock. Its brassbound corner still glinted, faintly as a glow-worm, after two hundred years.

Alastair's heart began to race. He had a rope in his bag too, a strong rope for scrambling about in caves. He could tie it round the hawthorn trunk – his knots were pretty good – and climb down into the well. There he would retrieve the box, the precious box; for somewhere among its hoard of gold was the clipped guinea that would take him back into the past. Finding the exact coin might be difficult, but he could try them all in the Gable Room crack, one after another, until his own world dissolved, and he was back with Martha.

It was possible. It was more than possible.

With trembling hands, he drew out his rope. It was fine nylon cord, very strong. He swung it round the tree, making a taut loop; and all the time he was letting himself picture her thin, tragic face, with its snow-pale cheeks, and storm-dark eyes, and the curling tangle of her hair.

'Martha!' he called softly. 'I'm coming!'

And then, he stopped.

He remembered the last time he'd called out those words to her. He'd been frantically crawling up the staircase, knowing she was in an agony of fear, desperate for James's safety.

If he put the coin back in the crack, as he wanted, wouldn't he be sentencing her to suffer all that torment again?

He dropped on to a stone, and sat still, thinking. Could he call her back from whatever far place she had reached? Much as he longed to see her, was it fair?

Like the guinea and the counterpoise in the excise-man's scales, he weighed the two possibilities. Dark Owlsnap against Quarmby Hall; her fears for James against his own aching wish to see her; a re-run of her anguish, or a lifelong blank where she had been?

'*If we could get away* ...' Suddenly he knew he couldn't deny her what she really wanted. She meant too much to him.

He untied the rope, coiled it, and dropped it into his bag. He put the torch in too, and gently moved the bent ferns back, to cover the mouth of the Bottomless Well.

It would be a good thing if Dad concreted it over. Mitt the Kitt had provided the perfect excuse for suggesting it. Then no one would be able to find the coins, and disturb Martha's peace. No one. Ever.

So this really was good-bye. He stood for a moment at the edge of the Bottomless Well. Then slowly he began to push through the brambles towards the house.